An Heir For The Billionaire

By

Terry Towers

Dedication:

This book is dedicated to my mother who passed away on Oct 14, 2012 after a year and a half long battle with lung cancer. She was my biggest cheerleader and my best friend and is greatly missed.

It is also dedicated to those who are currently battling or have battled cancer in the past and their loved ones.

Finally, it is dedicated to my readers. Much love to all of you and thank you for supporting me and by purchasing this book helping fund the Canadian Cancer Society.

Regards,
Terry

*****

To check out how much we've raised through our "Steamy Reading For A Cause" promotion please check out our website at www.elixaeverett.com

An Heir For The Billionaire

Copyright 2013 by Terry Towers
Cover by: Terry Towers

This book is a work of fiction. Any resemblance to persons, living or dead, or places, events or locales is purely coincidental. The characters are productions of the authors imagination and used fictitiously.

Chapter 1

"Ohhhh no, no. I can't do that." Looking up at the work schedule Katrina Alexander gave her head a soft shake. Her blonde ponytail swung back and forth behind her head, like a whip lashing out in mid-air.

"Why? You doing something that night?"

Katrina sighed tugging at her black necktie, loosening it. There was a brief moment of silence between them, as she tried to collect her thoughts before turning her attention over to her closest friend and co-worker Farrah Glover. "No, I can't. I mean... I can. But I don't want to."

"Why? It's a high school reunion, those are the easiest jobs. People tip bigger than normal trying to impress everyone else and it's a buffet so there's not much clean-up. And we get to work it together. We got lucky baby."

With her tie loosened she pulled it up and over her head. Crumbling the tie in her hand she stuffed it into the front pocket of her black vest. "Yeah, but it's for *my* high school."

"Oh, so you're attending then?"

"Nope." Grabbing at the black fabric hair-tie that was keeping her long blonde locks secure behind her head, she gave it a tug freeing her silken strands. Flipping her head forward, she shook her hair free. As it straightened out, it cascaded down her shoulders and back.

"Why?"

Katrina took a step back and motioned towards her server uniform. "Farrah, I'm twenty-eight years old, single, and a banquet server at a hotel. Besides, I was never all that popular in high school anyhow." She shrugged. "The only reason I'd go to begin with would be to gloat about how wonderful my life is and, well, as you can see it leaves a lot to be desired."

"Oh, come on. There must be someone that you'd like to see again."

Katrina turned and began to walk down the hallway in the direction of the car park, Farrah hot on her heels. "Geez. I don't know."

"What about that guy you dated?"

"Damon?"

"Yeah. Don't you want to see what he's done with his life?"

Katrina paused in her tracks as she was teleported back to the day he told her he was leaving Bangor, Maine to go to school in California: the day he'd broken her heart. He'd claimed that they'd keep in touch and they'd find a way to move her out there as well, once he got settled in, but there was never enough money and he became consumed with his studies. Daily calls turned to every few days then to once a week. After a year of trying to make a long distance relationship work they'd thrown in the towel.

She often wondered about him. She'd heard through the grapevine he owned a company and moved to New York, but whether it was true or not, she had no clue. However, she couldn't help but wonder on whether he was now some hotshot, while she had remained in Bangor, making nothing of her life. It would be humiliating. The last thing she wanted was for him to find out about the mess she'd made of her life.

Reaching the back door of the hotel, she pulled it open while waiting for Farrah, who was not far behind, to catch up. "I would have loved to go, but the truth is; I'm embarrassed, Farrah. What if they've all made it in life, you know *doctors, lawyers, professionals.*" Katrina bent her head sheepishly before uttering her next few words. "What if they're *all* successful?"

Farrah edged in closer, patting her on the back for comfort. "Having a good job doesn't always make you successful *or* happy."

"I know, but it's not just about their careers…I'm sure most of them are probably married with wonderful kids and suburban homes; you know, with the white picket fence. Living the American dream."

"No one lives the American dream," Farrah interjected.

"I'd be humiliated to tell them I'm just a server, barely getting by and scared to answer my phone because of all the bill collectors calling."

Farrah tisked at her. "Oh, come on Katrina, give yourself some credit. You work hard, making an honest living. You're beautiful.

And although you may not realize it, you do have a lot going for you."

Katrina rolled her eyes in response.

"I'm serious. We make an honest living and there's nothing wrong with being a server. Listen honey, just because you're a server now, doesn't mean you'll be a server forever."

"You know, just last week I had to serve someone from my high school for a meeting breakfast banquet. She's a lawyer. She looked at me with sympathy, like I was the most pathetic thing on earth, and told me maybe one day I'd catch a break. Then she proceeded to gush about how wonderful her fiancé was while flashing me the gigantic rock on her finger. And she used to be a *friend* of mine in high school. Now I'd imagine that type of condescending attitude from someone I never got along with, but a friend..."

"I'm sure people like that are few and far between. Everyone is out of work these days. We're lucky we even have a job that pays the bills."

"*Barely* pays the bills you mean. I swear it feels like I'm begging for an extension on the rent more than I pay on time. I'm just sick of this shit, you know."

Farrah shrugged, as they approached Katrina's ancient yellow VW. "It'll get better. Gotta have some faith honey."

"Yeah." Opening the car door, Katrina slid in, reached across the seat and unlocked the passenger side for Farrah.

Once they were both in, seat belts secure, Katrina thrust the key into the ignition.

Click.

Frowning and getting a bad feeling in the bit of her stomach, Katrina tried the ignition a second time.

Click.

"Oh, you have got to be fucking kidding me!" She slammed her hands on the steering wheel in utter frustration.

*****

Damon stood and extended his hand to his long time friend and doctor, Gary Van Buren. "Thanks for coming by the office with the results Gary, I appreciate it. I've been swamped with work." He motioned to a chair across from his desk. "Please, have a seat."

"No worries Damon." Sitting, Dr. Van Buren pulled a file from his briefcase and using the case as a mobile desk on his lap, opened the file.

"So... Tell me. What's the results?"

"Well, just let me say that the surgery wasn't for nothing..."

Damon let out a low huff of air as he sat back in his chair. His right side suddenly began to ache, where the incision had been made and the lower lobectomy had been performed. While the incision had healed, he still felt some discomfort.

"So, I still have it, I assume."

"Yes. We didn't get it all. I'm sorry Damon. We can still see fine specks of it in the lymph nodes and chest."

Damon pushed his chair back, stood and made his way over to the bar he had set up in the corner of his office. Opening a bottle of scotch, he poured a couple of ounces into a shot glass and chugged it down. The liquid burned as it slid over his tongue and down his throat. He motioned towards the bottle. "Care to join me for a drink, Doc?"

"No thanks, Damon." Gary paused as if deciding on something. "You shouldn't be drinking Damon."

"Doctor, I've never smoked a cigarette. Never did any type of illegal drug. Eat healthy and work out five times a week and still got lung cancer at the age of twenty-nine. Pretty fucked up if you ask me. I think having a couple shots of scotch is the least of my problems at this point. Don't you?" Damon poured another drink and drank it down as he waited for the verdict. "So what do we do from here?"

Gary looked down at his files, studied them a moment and then met Damon's gaze. "I suggest we start chemotherapy in a couple of weeks, followed by radiation. And then go from there."

"What are my chances?"

Gary shifted uneasily in his chair.

"That bad, huh?"

"You see when we went in and did the lobectomy we thought it was a different type of tumour. One less aggressive. We didn't realize it was small stem cell..."

"How long Gary? If this treatment you have planned doesn't work. How long?" Damon made his way back to his chair. His mind was numb. He'd been bracing himself for this news, but hearing it was still none-the-less hard. Twenty-nine years old and he was facing death, possibly in the near future.

"Well, without treatment maybe a few months."

Fuck! Damon thrust a hand through his dark hair as he sat back into his tall-back black leather desk chair. "And with the treatment?"

"With the treatment, we may be able to cure you. Maybe not. It's a crapshoot to be honest, but it's a hell of a lot worse if you don't do the treatment."

"And with the treatment. What's the odds?"

Gary grimaced. "About twenty percent Damon. You're young and in good health so you have a fighting shot. I'm quite sure that it'll give you a solid year if not cured, but a year is much better than a few months."

One year to live. It seemed surreal to him, like he was caught in some nightmare and he was going to wake up at any minute and it would be over and he could get back to his life. Though when he thought more deeply about it the truth of the matter was that his life was rather one-dimensional. It consisted of work, building an empire that was worth billions and nothing else.

No wife. No children. No family. Not even any close personal relationships. He didn't even have someone to leave his empire too when he passed. If he let himself ponder on those things he'd be too depressed to even function. But he pushed those things to the back of his mind.

Damon's eyes fell on a letter from his former high school. The letter was an invitation to his ten year high school reunion. A soft smile touched his lips as he thought back to his high school days. Life was so much simpler back then. Hell, if he knew back then what he knew now maybe he'd have changed several decisions he'd made in his younger years.

"Damon?"

Damon lifted his eyes and met Gary's gaze. "Alright. Set it up."

Gary made a couple of notes in his files and thrust it back into his briefcase. Gary's brow furrowed as he noticed the letter for the reunion. "Your reunion coming up I see."

"Yeah. Not going though."

"When is it?"

"This weekend, in Bangor. I have a meeting Friday afternoon in LA and to be honest I'm not sure I'd be up to seeing people from my past again."

Gary leaned forward and caught Damon's gaze. "If you'd like my opinion, I think you should go Damon. I'm confident we can beat this, despite the odds, but I would suggest you start reconnecting with people and start *living* your life instead of continuing to consume yourself with work. Speaking as your friend and not your doctor - fuck work." He motioned to the lavish office. "You can't take it with you Damon."

"Work is the only thing keeping me sane Gary."

"I'm just saying. Don't waste the time you have left, just in case."

"I'll think about it."

"I really can't afford this, Farrah."

"I'll pay."

"You can't afford it either." Katrina examined the tight black crushed velvet dress from all angles in the full length mirror of the clothing boutique. The sweetheart neckline dipped low into her amble cleavage and the tight skirt fell to mid-thigh. It was simple, but had an air of elegance to it.

Farrah came up behind Katrina and caught her friend's eyes in the mirror.

"Look how it brings out your blue eyes. Add some smoky cat eye make-up and a pair of sexy stilettos and you'll be a knockout. It won't matter what you do for a living, or you're so broke that you can't afford to fix your car. You'll have every man there drooling and every woman green with envy."

"Exactly. I can't even afford to fix my car Farrah, so does it make sense to you for me to spend a hundred bucks on a dress?"

"Like I said; I'll lend you the money for the dress and the car repairs. I haven't maxed my VISA yet."

"But Damon isn't even going to be there anyhow and he's the only person I'd be even remotely interested in seeing."

"How do you know he's not going to be there?"

Katrina flushed, a guilty expression crossing her face. "I kinda snuck into Winnie's office and checked the reservation list."

"Well, he can always confirm at the last minute. Besides, Winnie already approved you the night off, so you have to go or she'll be pissed that you made her change the schedule for nothing. You know what kind of tight-ass she is about changing the schedule."

"Yeah... I suppose..."

A wide smile emerged on Farrah's lips; she knew she won. "Then it's settled."

"Alright. You win. If you'll stop harassing me about it I'll buy the dress and go. But I'm not promising I'll stay for the whole thing. More of a drop in for the dance, see what's going on, and leave. No dinner. Just the dance."

Chapter 2

"I'm so nervous you wouldn't believe it." Katrina spun around and stuck her hand out, palm down. "See." Her outstretched left hand vibrated slightly.

Farrah laughed and rolled her eyes. "Look. I'll be serving drinks the whole night, so if you need back-up, I'll be here. And at least you're at work. You can escape back here and hang with us at any time.

"I suppose." Katrina turned back around to peer at her reflection in the mirror of the hotel's employee bathroom. She had to admit she looked like an entirely different person with the dramatic make-up and new dress. And despite the nervousness, she *felt* good. People say that new clothing and a little bit of pampering can do a whole lot for a persons' self-esteem and as she stood there examining herself, she believed it.

"Thanks for convincing me to go. I think you're right. This might be good for me."

Farah grinned. "Told ya."

"Farrah, the guests are leaving the banquet area and beginning to arrive in the ballroom, I need you out serving the drinks and appetizers," Winnie called, from the other side of the bathroom door.

Katrina spun back around to face Farrah and gave her a quick hug. "Thanks."

"Anytime."

Katrina gave herself one more look in the mirror, looking for any flaws in her make-up, as Farrah left. None. Grabbing her velvet clutch she took a deep breath in and slowly released it calming her nerves. After giving herself a quick pep talk, she exited the bathroom and made her way to the front entrance of the ballroom.

As she approached the front entrance she immediately recognized the two women who were manning the front door passing out name tags to those who hadn't attended the dinner. Neither one of them had been all that friendly to her during high school. They'd been on the cheerleading squad and she'd been a nobody. But she supposed being a nobody had been better than being one of the untouchables.

Keeping her head held high and shoulders squared she approached the table. The two women looked up and examined her, their eyes surveying every detail of her appearance. After what felt like an eternity, they finally met her gaze and smiled, questioning expressions on her faces.

"Katrina Alexander," she explained. Looking down at the list she found her name and pointed a perfectly French manicured finger on her name. The manicure was yet another expense she hadn't wanted to take on, but Farrah had insisted she go all out, so she'd finally given in and splurged. Twenty-eight years old and still giving in to peer pressure, she was disappointed in herself.

"Ahhhh Katrina." The first woman began to scrawl her name on a white sticky nametag in black magic marker. "How have you been?" She gave Katrina a smile that was so fake it made her want to roll her eyes. She refrained, but it was hard.

She took a second to look a little further down the list and a shiver of anticipation shot down her spine when she saw Damon's name pencilled in and checked off. He must have called in at the last second. And he was here... Somewhere.

"Thank you." Taking the tag, she pressed it onto the left side of her chest and entered the ballroom, through an archway made of red and white balloons.

The lights in the ballroom were lowered and it was decorated similar to what the gym had looked like during their senior prom, in the school colours of red and white. A flood of memories came rushing back to her, most of which featured Damon. They'd been inseparable during high school, the couple voted most likely to be married and have children before they were twenty-five.

Don't get your hopes up. Chances are he's married with a mistress and four children by now. Even if he doesn't, it's not like anything other than catching up would take place anyhow.

She scanned the ballroom, eyeing each of the tall dark-haired men trying to find Damon. Some of the men looked slightly familiar, but many of them she didn't recognize. After taking time to scrutinize each of the men she found herself disappointed that unless his looks changed drastically over the years, he wasn't one of them. Letting out a loud sigh, Katrina made her way over to the bar and ordered a strawberry daiquiri.

He's already checked in so he must be around here somewhere.

"Here ya are, Katrina. On the house. You look beautiful by the way," the tall, sexy, mocha-skinned bartender said, passing her the daiquiri.

"Thanks Jerome."

Jerome leaned over the counter and gave her a smile that would normally have women swooning over him, which is why she always rejected him. She imagined he'd lost count of his conquests a long time ago. "So when we going out anyway?"

"Oh, Jerome. My guess is never."

"I'll keep asking," he warned.

"I'll keep saying no," she retorted laughing as she turned to leave.

"I'll have a scotch, on the rocks."

Katrina froze; the man's voice behind her was deep and sexy, and so familiar that it sent a shiver down her spine. Slowly, she turned back to the bar and there he was, in the flesh, as sexy as he had been the last day she'd seen him, almost ten years ago. She gulped down the lump forming in her throat as she watched him pay for his drink.

"Damon?" While asked as a question there was no doubt it was him. Six-foot-two, broad shoulders, dark hair and equally as dark eyes. Maybe it was the fine cut suit that fit him perfectly, or maybe it was the air of confidence and cockiness that he had about him now that made him heart-stopping sexy. She didn't know, but all the feelings she'd had for him a decade ago came crashing down on her, including the pain and hurt of their break-up.

His eyes immediately lit up with recognition as they caught hers. "Katrina?"

Katrina nodded.

Placing his drink on the bar he closed the distance between them and pulled her into a brief hug. Keeping her drink out of the way, she wrapped her free arm around his neck and held tight to him. She buried her face against his neck and his aftershave drifted to her, smelling of woods and spices. It drew her in, and she longed to stay in his warm embrace. But to her dismay, he ended the hug way too quickly and stepped away picking his scotch back up and taking a long drink.

"You look..." Damon took a moment to survey her, and she found herself grateful that she'd bought the new dress, including the fishnet thigh-high stockings. "I'm speechless. You look stunning Katrina. You've barely changed since I last saw you."

Katrina felt her cheeks grow warm and she lowered her gaze, feeling like a teenager again. "Thank you." After a moment, she lifted her blue eyes and smiled. On impulse she reached out and fingered the lapels of his suit jacket. The material was unbelievably soft under her fingertips. "You're looking pretty good yourself. The years seem to have been equally as kind to you."

His jaw clenched and she thought she saw a flash of sadness and regret in his eyes, but as quickly as it appeared, the look disappeared and a smile touched his lips. "I've done okay."

"By the way you used to work I would imagine you must be the big honcho at some multi-million dollar company by now. Living the dream."

His grin widened and he shrugged. "I've done okay."

Katrina's eyes followed his left hand as he raised his glass to take a sip of his scotch. No wedding ring or indication that there had been one there recently. A rush of relief and satisfaction flowed through her.

She opened her mouth to speak, but was interrupted by the president of their graduating class - Kirk Miller.

"Welcome everyone to the ten year reunion of South Haven High, class of 2003!"

Clapping and cheers erupted from the several hundred people who were in attendance. Katrina's eyes left the stage and Kirk to check out Damon, while he was distracted. She stood just above his shoulder, her 5'7 little more than six inches shorter than him. Sensing her eyes on him, he looked down at her and gave her a wink. Her heart fluttered and pulse raced at the gesture. She immediately shifted her gaze back to the stage, but could still feel his eyes on her.

Despite her eyes being on Kirk, whatever he was saying was lost on her. Her mind was focused on the tremors rushing through her at the feeling of him watching her. She wondered if he had a girlfriend or woman at home. And where was home? There was so much she wanted to know, she silently prayed Kirk would wind up his long-winded speech soon so she could get back to Damon. Apparently, Kirk liked to hear himself talk just as much now as he had when they were younger.

"And now, I see that the prom king and queen are here tonight. So let's kick off the night with the king and queen dancing to the same song they danced to all those years ago."

Here Without you, by 3 Doors Down began to play and with a little coaxing the former king and queen joined together in the center of the dance floor. Neither one seemed overly impressed to be forced to dance together, which made Katrina wonder what had transpired between them to cause such a rift.

"He's gay."

"Huh?" Katrina's brows furrowed as she tore her eyes from the couple to meet Damon's.

"That's why they're slightly hostile towards each other. He left her for a man not to long after graduation. She took it hard."

Katrina's blue eyes widened and her jaw went slack. "No way!"

Damon grinned and nodded his confirmation. "Yes way."

People began to pair up and join the king and queen on the dance floor.

Turning towards her, Damon took her daiquiri from her hand and extended his hand to her. "Will you join me Kat?"

Katrina looked down at his outstretched hand and hesitated. Looking back up into his dark eyes she saw the regret in them, a silent apology and request for forgiveness. He was extending an olive branch to her, so how could she not accept?

"Please, Katrina."

"I'd love to," she responded taking his hand. His hand closed around hers, eclipsing her small on into his larger one as he led her to the dance floor. He led her to the side of the dance floor, away from the other embracing couples and then pulled her into his arms.

She twirled once, laughing softly, her blonde locks whipping around her head as she twirled and then slipped into his arms, sliding her hands up his chest and locking her fingers behind his neck. He immediately pulled her close, and she found herself amazed at how familiar it felt to be in his arms again. The years seemed to peel back and she was transported in time ten years to when life was simple and they were in love.

*****

Katrina buried her face against his neck, as Damon pulled her closer. Her body felt so good against him, it had been a while since he'd been with a woman and he'd forgotten how good it felt to hold someone he cared about so closely.

He'd thought about her more times than he could count over the years. Whenever he'd feel the hint of loneliness she'd appear in his mind. She'd been so sweet and carefree. It didn't matter how crazy his ideas had been or how impossible his dreams were, she'd always supported him. Even when he got accepted to Stanford, she was the one to tell him to go, even though he knew it was the last thing she'd wanted him to do.

A rush of guilt and regret came crashing over him, hitting him like a slug to the stomach. "I'm sorry Kat."

She tensed in his arms and pulled back to look him in the eye. Her brow furrowed. "For what?"

"For leaving you behind."

She smiled, but the smile was weak at best. "It was for the best." She looked down and fingered the lapel of his suit jacket. "We had different paths..."

The song switched up to *U Got It Bad,* by Usher.

"No, I was selfish. I was young and wanted to conquer the world. I didn't realize that I already had what was most important in life. I've never again found a love like what I had with you."

She opened her mouth to comment and then snapped it shut. Damon cursed himself for coming on too strong. He'd been doing a lot of self-reflection over the past little while and despite the sense of accomplishment he got whenever he took over a new company; the truth of the matter was that he'd never been truly happy since he moved out of Bangor and away from her. When he considered his life, he had four years of pure happiness and they were all due to her.

Damon pulled her back into his arms. He lowered his nose to her hair and took in the scent of her shampoo - apple. "Your hair even smells the same."

Katrina laughed and glanced up at him. "I'm not one for change. I can't believe you remember what shampoo I used to use."

"I remember a lot of things, Kat."

She lowered her gaze, a blush colouring her cheeks. "Me too. Every time I go to the park and wind up at the lookout and I remember the night you first told me..." Her voice trailed off and her blush deepened.

"That I loved you," Damon finished off for her.

She nodded.

"I did Kat, but my ambition got in the way." He caught her chin in his hand and tilted her face up so her eyes caught him. "It was real. I don't doubt that for an instant."

A look crossed her face that reminded him so much of the eighteen year old young woman he'd foolishly left that it left him winded. The music ended and neither of them noticed until the couples around them began to break up as the tempo increased.

With great reluctance, Damon released his grip on Katrina and stepped back, however, he kept her hand securely in his. "Can I make a confession?" He asked as he led her from the dance floor.

She looked unsure. He was overloading her, he knew this, but he needed to say what was on his mind and in his heart. He didn't have the luxury of time any longer.

"I'm still trying process your apology," she admitted.

"Come with me." He led her through the ballroom and out into the foyer.

"Where are we going?"

"A place a little quieter and less crowded. I rented a room here yesterday afternoon and did a little exploring last night. I found a beautiful little spot..."

"Ahhh. The gardens. You're right. They're beautiful."

Damon laughed. "Guess you've been doing some exploring here as well. Are you also staying here tonight?"

Katrina paused, her eyes lowering and a faint blush touching her cheeks. "Not exactly."

Damon cocked a brow at her and chuckled. "What do you mean by *not exactly*?"

"Well, I sort of work here."

"Oh?" Coming up to the doors leading to the gardens, he opened it up and stepped back, letting her enter before him.

"Yeah."

"What do you do?"

Chapter 3

Katrina's insides were turning to jelly as the memories continued to compound. Damon's confession only added to the turmoil brewing within her. She had no idea that seeing him would have such a powerful effect on her. If she'd known she may have reconsidered coming tonight.

"Kat?" Damon prompted.

"Not all of us were able to do well for ourselves out of high school and leave this place Damon," she snapped and then cringed at the look of surprise on his face at her reaction.

"Did I say something that implied that working here was a bad thing? If I had it wasn't my intention."

Sighing, Katrina raked a hand through her hair, embarrassed she'd gotten so touchy with him. "No. I'm sorry. I just..." Walking over to the seven foot tall marble fountain in the center of the gardens she sat down on the white marble bench, crossing one shapely leg over the other. The flow of the water trickling down the sculpture and into the base helped soothe her slightly frazzled state.

With a frown creasing his brow Damon walked over to the fountain and sat next to her. "What's wrong? Maybe I can help?"

Giving him a rueful smile, she shook her head. She began to finger the lace at the hem of her skirt trying to distract herself from the slew of mixed emotions flowing through her. "I'm being overly sensitive. I'm sorry. Just seeing you and seeing the others... Well, it makes me feel like I've wasted the last ten years."

Damon covered her small delicate hands with one of his and hooked the index finger of his other hand under her chin tilting her eyes up to meet his. "Why? Why would you think such a thing?"

Her heart rate accelerated and another wave of emotions flooded her as she looked deep into his dark brown eyes. It occurred to her that perhaps the problem was that she never really got the closure that she needed. On some level she'd hoped maybe they'd work it out at a later date. They'd made so many promises to each other all those years ago and none of them came to be.

She fingered the expensive material of his jacket lapel a moment as she gathered her thoughts. "I'm a banquet server Damon. I can't pay my bills and haven't even come close to feeling for a man the way I..." She stopped herself from finishing the sentence, feeling foolish. Who held a touch for a high school crush for ten years? No one. Just her.

"There's nothing wrong with being a banquet server Kat. Nothing at all."

She huffed and gave him a forced smile. "Things just seemed so much easier back then. And I guess I didn't realize how much I've resented the life that I've made for myself until the past few days when I did a full autopsy of it."

"You know, I've done a similar autopsy recently."

"Oh."

"Yeah. You wanna know how many women I've had relationships with since high school?"

Katrina couldn't even harbour a guess if she wanted to. He was educated, sexy-as-sin, successful, she guessed too many to count. She shook her head.

"None."

Katrina laughed and gave him a swat on the shoulder. "Oh, come on. A guy like you."

He grinned cocking a brow up at her. "A guy like me?"

"Yeah. Good looking. Too smart for his own good and it's blatantly apparent you've done well for yourself. How could you not?"

Damon shrugged. "When at Stanford, my studies were number one. When I graduated, work and building my company was my focus. I always thought I'd have time later on in life to find someone and have a family."

Katrina rolled her eyes at him, laughing lightly at the gloomy nature of his comment. "Oh come on, you have lots of time for that. Women have a shorter expiration date on having children than men."

He grinned, amusement gleaming in his eyes. "I'm not even going to comment on that statement."

"Such a smart guy." Her mood lifted. "So guess that means no children, huh?"

The amusement in his eyes dimmed and the sadness she thought she'd seen earlier flashed in his eyes, but only for a moment and then amusement reappeared. "None. You?"

She shook her head. "None."

"And do you want kids?"

"I always did. I just have to.... ya know. Find a man. Get married. And all that before I can get to the children part."

"At least the man part anyhow."

Katrina grinned. "Well, a man isn't necessity needed."

Damon laughed. "We do carry an essential ingredient to the baby making formula."

"You know what I mean silly." Leaning into him, Katrina gave him a little nudge to his right side. To her surprise his breath hitched and he flinched, his smile fading.

Her eyes widened in surprise at his reaction. "Oh-my-God, I didn't think I nudged you that hard. I'm sorry Damon!"

His jaw clenched and a smile returned to his lips. "Nah, you just took me by surprise. I'm fine."

Not convinced she reached to pull at his shirt to get a look at his side and he jerked backwards away from her, taking her hands in his. "I'm fine Kat..." he gave her a stern look, a look he used to give her when they were younger when he had no intention of discussing something further. "Really."

He's lying, a voice in the back of her head told her. Despite the years that had passed, she could still tell when he was lying, but she didn't press the topic. If there was something going on that he wanted to share with her, he would, in his own time.

"Okay."

He gave her hands a light squeeze. "I'm fine," he repeated.

****

Damon's side was hurting like a bitch, and he had to force himself to keep from wincing. It had been healing well, but she'd nailed him right on the incision. He could tell she suspected he was keeping something from her, but the last thing he wanted was to reconnect with her and within the first hour of being with her toss out the "Big C" news. If she was anything like she was when they were younger - and from their brief discussion so far he suspected she was - then she'd become sick with worry. He wanted to enjoy being with her, not suddenly be a target of pity. No, he'd keep that information tightly guarded unless he had to fess up.

He glanced down at her hands in his. They were so petite, his large ones eclipsing them completely. He unconsciously stroked the palms of her hands with his thumbs.

Katrina inhaled sharply, drawing his eyes back to hers. There was a tint of desire in her sapphire blue eyes. His eyes lowered to her lips, painted pink and glossed. The ache in his side was forgotten as his mind became distracted with a different kind of ache.

Her lips beckoned to him. He wondered if she'd kiss him in the way she had years ago, with such passion. He could still remember the way she'd sigh against his mouth as she pressed herself against him.

"So no husband, fiancé, boyfriend?"

She shook her head, running her tongue along her lower lip - enticing him.

"So if I were to do something a little crazy like kiss you..." Releasing one of her hands, he slowly raked a hand through her golden locks, watching the strands fall from his fingertips - strand by strand. She closed her eyes and sighed, her soft sigh sounding like music to his ears and bringing back memories; memories that he'd savoured over the years in the odd instances where he let himself think of something other than work.

Katrina opened her eyes. "I'd say sometimes you need to do something crazy from time to time."

Damon smiled as he lowered his lips to hers. As he drew closer to her the smell of her perfume drifted up to his nose and spurred his arousal. He ghosted his lips across hers and a sweet, soft sigh that sent his dick into a frenzy escaped her. He fought to hold himself back, wanting to savour the feel of her soft lips against his, before deepening the kiss.

Placing her palms against his chest, she leaned into him, parting her lips with a soft moan and inviting him in. Damon accepted the invitation, savouring her sweet response as their tongues touched. Her hands fisted the front of his shirt and she moved closer.

She was such a temptation to him - she always had been and he suspected always would be. With great reluctance Damon ended the kiss before he got carried away. There was no doubt that the attraction was still alive and well between them, despite the years that have passed.

As he pulled back and their eyes locked an idea came to him. It was crazy, but then again maybe crazy was what he needed. He might as well take some chances, he had nothing to lose. It was painfully evident that she wanted a new life, and he needed the assurance that his years of blood, sweat and tears didn't go to waste. The more that he thought about it, the less insane the idea became. All he needed to do was convince Katrina to marry him and have his baby...

Chapter 4

"Damon?" Katrina frowned at Damon's sudden intense and distant expression. It wasn't exactly the type of expression she'd have expected after him kissing her and it made her uneasy.

The distant expression faded and he was back to her, giving her a soft, sexy smile. "I'm sorry. Got distracted for a moment."

She returned his smile with some hesitation. "Good distracted I hope..."

Damon brushed his knuckles against her cheek. "Very good."

"So how long are you staying here? I don't even know where you live yet or what you even do for a living."

He opened his mouth to answer and paused. "You know, I think I just had a change in plans and I'll be staying until Monday morning."

Because of me? She chewed at her lower lip and wondered if she was wise to hope he was staying for her. He'd broken her heart once already and even though being in Damon's presence brought back many good memories of the past, the truth was she didn't know the new Damon.

So learn, a voice in the back of her mind urged her.

"Were you planning on leaving in the morning?"

His grin widened. "It was all in limbo depending..."

"On?"

Movement from inside the hotel caught her eye over Damon's shoulder. Trying to look natural, she leaned a little to the left and had to fight a smile from forming on her lips at the sight of Farrah on the other side of the window, pointing to Damon and waving her hand in front of her as if she were going to faint.

So hot! Farrah mouthed, giving her the A-ok sign with her fingers.

Damon began to answer, but his words were lost on her as she tried to motion for Farrah to go away without Damon noticing. Her distress over Farrah watching only spurred Farrah into more inappropriate motions. Nodding towards Damon's back Farrah began to press her tongue against her cheek while making jerking motions with her hand to her mouth.

"Oh-my-God, I'm going to kill her," Katrina growled. She'd meant to only think the words, but to her horror she'd verbalized her thoughts, breaking Damon from whatever it was he was saying.

"Who?" Frowning Damon turned around and froze as he watched Farrah continue the obscene gesture.

Being spotted Farrah immediate stopped, blushed slightly and gave them a timid half-wave. Not waiting for them to return the greeting she scurried off and out of sight.

With his head cocked and an eyebrow raised, Damon turned back to Katrina. "Friend of yours?"

It was Katrina's turn to blush, a deep crimson. "I ummmm. See. Well..."

Damon patiently waited as she stumbled over her words, a quizzical expression pasted on his handsome features.

"Well. Yeah. But. See." *Oh dear God*, she groaned inwardly. "She feels I don't get out enough and date and..."

"Get laid," Damon offered, with a twinkle of humour in his eyes.

Lowering her eyes Katrina covered her face with her hand. This had to be one of the most embarrassing moments she'd had to endure in a long, long time - if ever.

"You know. I was hoping that maybe we could just hang out this weekend, maybe reconnect. But I'm sure we could fit that in as well."

Damon's light chuckling prompted her to bite the bullet and lower her hand to peer up at him. "She was just messing around," Katrina attempted to explain.

He stopped laughing, but the amused grin remained on his face. "I figured as much."

"Which brings me to my question for you."

"Which is?" The amusement in his expression increased.

She paused, not sure if she was being bold in confronting him or being egotistical to think he'd do something like come home for a reunion just for her. But she had to ask the question. "Did you come here just to see me?"

His eyes locked with hers once again, and she felt the same shiver of anticipation run through her that she'd felt when he'd kissed her. She waited on bated breath.

"You are the *sole* reason for me being here."

"But why?" She reached out to him and fingered the soft cotton of his black button-down shirt. She really loved the material - so soft - and gave her a reason to touch him, even if briefly. "I mean, if you wanted to see me then you could have called. It's been ten years. Anytime." Another bout of hurt hit her. If he still wanted her after all these years then why didn't he come back for her? She wanted to say it didn't bother her, but it did.

Damon sighed and lifted his hands up, palms out and shrugged. "I don't know Katrina. I suppose a part of me was scared you'd refuse to talk to me. And I've been focused on work, way too focused, I know this now. I've had some *very* messed up priorities."

"So what changed it now?"

Damon paused, his expression darkening, indecision flashing in his eyes. After a moment a smile spread across his lips. "Things change."

Their eyes locked and a moment passed between them.

"Have you had supper? You didn't go to the reception did you?"

Katrina shook her head. "Nope and I am."

Damon stood and extended his hand to her, "Come on. Let's get out of here."

*****

"Now, be forewarned my secretary ordered the vehicle. Not me. I wouldn't drive anything so pretentious in Bangor," Damon explained as they entered the car park attached to the hotel.

Katrina frowned. "Pretentious?"

Damon chuckled. "Yeah. Pretentious." They rounded the corner and Katrina's eyes caught sight of what had to be the car he was speaking of, a candy apple red Ferrari. It stuck out like a sore thumb, surrounded by assortment of economy cars and SUV's in the parking garage.

"Wow. You're driving that?"

Walking over to the passenger side of the car, Damon unlocked it and assisted her into the low sitting car. "Yup."

Katrina was surprised at his dismissive attitude towards the vehicle. It was gorgeous. She settled back in the black leather seat. It was so lavish and comfortable. Her eyes scanned the interior of the car in awe.

"You don't like it?" she asked as he opened the driver's door and slid in next to her, starting the car. The powerful engine roared to life, sending a tremor of excitement through her. This was the first time she'd ever been in a Ferrari. So cool.

He placed his hand on the gearshift preparing to put it into drive. "Oh I do. It's a fantastic car. But it just sticks out too much here, like I'm trying to impress someone or something. Becky must have assumed I'd want it since it's what I drive home." He threw the car into first gear and pulled out of the parking slot.

"At home?"

Damon glanced at her out of the corner of his eye as he negotiated the parking garage and exited onto the street. "Yeah, I live in New York now."

"Really?" Her spirits lifted. He was on the east coast. Granted it was about a ten hour drive away, but still close. If they hit it off... She stopped her train of thought in its tracks. The last thing she wanted to do was look past the weekend and get disappointed.

"Yeah. Moved there a few years ago. It made much more sense to be there from a business perspective."

"And so do you live right in Manhattan or in Jersey."

He glanced over at her and smiled. "Manhattan. Near Central Park."

Katrina was impressed. He drove a Ferrari and lived near Central Park? He really did do very well for himself; at least it appeared to be that way. "Wow, that's impressive. Business must be good."

He flashed a sexy smile at her that made her heart rate accelerate. "I guess you could say I've done okay for myself," he conceded. "In some areas of my life anyhow." His gaze dropped from hers moving lower to her chest, making the heat flare up between her legs.

She turned her eyes away and frowned. "Where are we going to eat anyhow?"

"Is Mama Mays still open?"

"Believe it or not, it is." Katrina smiled at the mention of Mama Mays. Mama Mays was the little mom and pop pizza place on the border of Bangor and Brewer that they used to eat at every noon hour when in high school. A rush of memories filled her head and her smile widened. Without thinking she placed her hand over his on the gear shift, lacing her fingers with his.

His hand tightened on hers, causing her to glance over at him, catching his gaze for a brief moment before he shifted his eyes back to the road. "So I was thinking we could take a little trip down memory lane?"

I already am, Katrina mused. "What do you have in mind?"

"I was thinking that we have ourselves a couple of slices of pizza, maybe a Coke and then go to the lookout."

Cocking her head to the side, Katrina grinned. "Do you plan on seducing me with pizza and taking me parking, Damon Garratt?"

Damon gave her hand another squeeze, downshifting. "We could forgo the pizza if you like and skip to the parking."

He glanced over at her and caught her eyes, a mischievous gleam shone in his eyes - the same gleam he used to get when he was teasing her when they were young. No matter how much things had changed, they stayed the same. She certainly wasn't expecting there to be such a familiarity. It was both arousing and unsettling.

"We can't forgo Mama May's now that you have me excited over it!"

Arriving at Mama May's, the parking lot was virtually empty, which was unusual for a Friday night. As Damon slid the car into a parking slot, Katrina couldn't help but notice eyes examining the car.

"You're right."

"Huh?" Damon parked the car and glanced over at her, eyebrow raised.

"The car sticks out. I think every set of eyes in the area is on us."

*****

Opening the car door, Damon offered his hand to Katrina assisting her out of the low sitting car. "Does Mama May still work?" He doubted it; she'd been nearing sixty when they were in high school.

Katrina grinned. "Believe it or not. She does."

"Wow."

"Her son, Richard, more or less took over for her a few years ago though."

She straightened and adjusted the skirt of her dress that had risen dangerously high on her thighs. Not that he minded - not one bit.

"Hey!"

Damon's eyes lifted, a brow cocked. "Huh?"

She pointed two fingers towards her eyes scowling, but there was amusement in her eyes. "My eyes are here, buddy."

Damon grinned. "You wore the dress, woman. He nudged her out of the way with his hip and closed the car door, locking it. "Can't blame a guy for looking."

"Not like you haven't seen them before," she teased, looking up at him with a hint of seduction in her gaze, as he took her hand on his and they made their way into the pizzeria.

Damon's dick jerked in his pants. He remembered alright. The years hadn't dimmed the memories of her silky thighs, or the soft sighs and moans she'd make whenever he spread her legs and indulged in her. He gritted his teeth and gave his head a quick shake, trying to clear the memories from his mind, partly scared the building erection in his pants would be visible to her.

As they entered the pizzeria, the succulent smells of cheese and pepperoni greeted their noses and he found his stomach grumbling. The place hadn't changed in ten years. He looked over at the booths, still red vinyl, but just more worn and cracked. A couple had red duct tape covering the cracks.

Memories came rushing back to him, punching him into the gut, forcing him to remember all the good times he had, before he allowed himself to become consumed with wealth and building his empire. To his surprise, he felt himself growing emotional - something he hadn't allowed himself to do since he first found out about the cancer. Sure, life hadn't been perfect when he'd been young, being tossed from foster home to foster home, but he had his share of good times - most of which involved Katrina.

"Damon?" A tug on his hand and Katrina's soft voice once again pulled him from his trip down memory lane.

Damon fought back the emotion and looked down into Katrina's concerned face.

"Are you okay?" She tightened her grip on his hand, her frown deepening.

"Yeah, of course." His eyes gave the pizzeria another scan. "Memories. Ya know?"

She nodded and gave him a smile. Her eyes surveyed the restaurant as his had. "Yeah. Lots."

"Katrina sweetie!" A soft voice exclaimed coming out from the kitchen. Damon turned his attention towards the kitchen and to his shock and amusement; an older version of the May he remembered came rushing from the kitchen and around the counter. Her hair had turned completely white and was pulled up into a bun at the top of her head. She'd also gained a few pounds, giving her the sweet grandmotherly look. "Haven't seen you in ages dear."

May pulled Katrina into a hug. "Where have you been hiding yourself?" She took a step back, but kept Katrina at arm's length. "You look beautiful. And who's this handsome man of yours?" May's blue eyes lifted their gaze to meet Damon's and narrowed.

Damon could see the wheels turning in her head as recognition slowly began to emerge, lighting up her eyes. "Well, I'll be... Damon Garratt!" She released Katrina and pulled Damon into a motherly embrace. "I can't believe it." As she held onto him, her hold not nearly as strong as she intended, the smell of baby power drifted to his nose.

She pulled away from him and took a few steps back to eye them both. A large smile emerged on her lips, delight in her eyes and she clapped lightly. "Are you two kids back together?"

Not sure what to say, Katrina spoke up. "No. Damon just came to town for the reunion."

May's face fell. "Awwww. I always thought you kids were perfect together." She directed her attention to Damon. "Are you with anyone?"

Damon shook his head and grinned. "No, Ma'am."

"Kids? Ex-wife?"

Again, Damon shook his head. "No, Ma'am."

Her face lit up again. "Then you two have a second chance."

Damon looked down at Katrina. Sensing his eyes on her she looked up and caught his gaze, her face reddening. "I think I'd like that Mrs. May," Damon stated.

"Oh, wonderful." She clapped again. "Let me get you two a pizza. Meat right?"

Laughing Damon confirmed with a nod. *How does she remember that?* He mouthed down to Katrina.

She didn't respond, but grinned. It didn't seem to surprise her at all.

Chapter 5

"Oh-my-God, Damon! I'm thinking this was a really bad idea," Katrina groaned out, through chattering teeth. It felt like her spine was going to be pushed up through her mouth as the Ferrari bounced and bumped over the dips of the dirt road leading the to Look-out.

The words had barely gotten out of her mouth when a loud scraping noise sounded from under the car. She grimaced.

Damon laughed. "Don't worry, it's insured."

"I think they have limitations due to reasonable use on that insurance though." They hit another dip, heard another angry grating sound from under the car and Katrina yelped, her head bouncing against the roof of the car.

"You okay?"

"Yeah." She rubbed her head a moment and then gripped the seat, praying for it to end. He reached over and touched her leg, just above the knee and she immediately felt her desire for him flare up.

Just when she thought she couldn't handle another moment of the rough ride, the car reached the summit and drove into the clearing, which overlooked all of Bangor. Katrina let out a sigh of relief falling back into the seat as Damon parked the car and shut off the engine.

He looked over at her giving her a sheepish grin. "Sorry about the rough ride. A Ferrari isn't exactly made for off-roading."

"It's okay. I was considering getting a new spine anyhow." Undoing her seat belt, Karina stretched and wiggled in the seat attempting to work out the kinks the rough ride caused within her.

Chuckling Damon got out of the car and walked around the front of the car. Katrina watched him walking around the car, taking a moment to admire him. He walked with such power and authority; it sent another rush of arousal through her. She squirmed in the seat as the heat between her legs grew more intense.

"Care to join me outside. It's a beautiful night," Damon asked opening her door and offering her his hand. She took his extended hand and as she got out her dress inched its way up her thighs. She noticed his gaze quickly lower to her legs and then just as quickly back up to meet hers.

"I noticed that," Katrina teased pulling at the hem of her skirt as she straightened.

"Noticed what?" He feigned ignorance, but the mischievous gleam in his dark eyes told her that he knew *exactly* what she was referring to.

"Checking out my legs." She stepped out of the way so he could close the car door.

"They're incredible legs."

Katrina laughed, giving her head a shake. "You're not even going to pretend to deny it."

Damon grinned. "Nope."

Taking her hand, he led her over to the old, wooden railing at the edge of the cliff. Side-by-side, they both leaned over it and took in the spectacular sight below them. Millions of lights sparkled below them, lighting up the otherwise dark night sky.

"I'd forgotten how beautiful it was up here," Katrina whispered.

"You haven't been up here lately?"

Katrina shook her head, her blonde hair swaying behind her. "Not for a while."

"Really?"

She tilted her head and looked up at him. "Well, it was our spot. It kinda brings back memories." Her face flushed as she remembered her first time - with him - in his beat up Ford Mustang.

Taking her hand Damon laced his fingers through hers. "What?" His eyes searched hers seeking out the reason for her embarrassment.

The heat in her cheeks deepened. "I was just remembering that old black Mustang you had back then."

Damon threw his head back and laughed. "Yeah that car was so old and beat up it was a damned miracle it worked."

"And remembering what happened in that car..." She was surprised at how vividly she remembered that night. The memories had faded over the years, but Damon being so close brought those memories in eerie detail. "I was so nervous."

His fingers tightened in hers and he closed the short distance between their bodies. "Want to hear a confession?"

Katrina looked up at him, an eyebrow cocked. "Confession?"

"Yeah. I know you thought that I'd had sex before. But I hadn't."

Frowning, Katrina turned to face him, her hip leaning against the railing. "But what about Amber Heiss? I thought..."

Damon shook his head. "No, we never did. People assumed and neither one of us corrected them."

She touched the lapel of his suit jacket, stroking it with her fingertips. "Why didn't you tell me?"

Damon shrugged. "Cause I was the man. I was supposed to be the experienced one."

"We were only sixteen. It wouldn't have mattered..." He'd seemed so sure and secure when they'd been together. The first time had hurt more than she'd anticipated, but she'd later discovered that part of the pain would have been because he'd been much bigger than most men - something she hadn't realized at the tender age of sixteen. But he'd been so gentle. He'd taken his time even though it was painfully evident it was killing him not to take what he'd wanted.

She pressed her palms against his chest; her fingers tracing the contours of muscle under the soft cotton shirt, the muscle flinched under her fingertips. Her eyes lowered and followed the trail of her fingertips. While they were teenagers Damon had been well-built, but she could tell he'd really filled out; his body strong and toned. She was aching to see what the new and improved Damon looked like without his clothing.

Damon slipped a hand into her hair, and raked his fingers through her locks from her scalp to the tip. She closed her eyes and sighed softly, loving the delicious pull of the strands.

"What are you thinking?"

His voice was deep and soft, cutting into her thoughts. She looked up and discovered his lips were a couple of inches from hers. She inhaled deeply and his cologne filled her nostrils. Her need for him was quickly increasing. Normally she wasn't the type of woman who craved a man upon first meeting them. She needed to make an emotional connection, before her body would react in such a way, but this was Damon. *Her* Damon.

The Damon that at one time had promised you forever and then left you, breaking your heart, the voice in the back of her mind reminded her. She ignored the voice as his lips lowered to hers. Slipping her hands up his chest, she laced her fingers behind his neck and pressed herself against him.

The feel of his warm, rock solid body next to hers felt good - too good. She parted her lips in a soft sigh and he deepened the kiss. Their tongues touched, sending a jolt of electric pleasure through her, causing her to rub against him, her stomach rubbing against the hardening ridge of his shaft.

He shifted his position, pressing her against the railing. The cool wood of the railing pressed into her shoulder blades and lower back, in contrast to the heat of his body. Damon's hands slid down to her ass and he cupped her ass cheeks in his hands, pulling her tighter to him.

Her tongue duelled with his, fuelling the fire between her legs. Her panties began to dampen as her desire rose, causing her to wiggle against him, attempting to relieve the building pressure.

Keeping his lips to hers, he groaned and then lifted her up. Her legs immediately wrapped around his waist and she held tight to him as he turned with her in his arms and carried her over to the car. The skirt of her dress slid up her hips and bunched around her waist. As he set her down onto the hood of the car, the cool metal of the red hood shocked her as it came in contact with her bare thighs and lace covered ass. She squealed, pulling her lips from his and giggling.

Damon pulled back, his dark eyes flaring with hunger.

"The car. It's kinda... Cool."

Damon's gaze lowered and his jaw clenched as he peered upon her black lace panties fully visible to him - an erotic contrast to the candy apple red hood of the car. To her dismay he straightened up and took a step back.

She was about to reach for him, to bring him back down to her. Her body was longing to feel his again and the coolness was irrelevant. Her pussy throbbed, her juices saturating the lace between her legs. Her eyes lowered to the front of his pants and her breath caught in her throat as she gazed upon his massive erection. He shrugged off his suit jacket and then reached around her.

"Lift up."

Placing her hands to her sides, she pushed her rear up and he slid his jacket under her bottom. "Are you sure, I'm ummmm...."

She chewed at her lower lip. She could only imagine how expensive the jacket was, considering how turned on she was she knew her juices would end up dripping onto it.

He cocked a brow up at her and a grin began to emerge on his lips. He leaned back down, spread her legs and lowered himself over her. He braced a hand on either side of head and caught her eyes. "You're what Kat?" He slid a hand between them and cupped her mound over her panties. "Wet for me?"

She nodded. "Very. And your jacket..."

"Will be fine." He captured her lips with his, as he fingered the lace at the waistband of her panties. His hand slipped lower, under the lace to cup her bare mound. She moaned and bucked against his hand. Her need for a man was becoming more than she'd ever experienced before. Maybe it was because she'd gone so long without being with a man, but she doubted it. She knew it was because it was him. She'd spent so many years re-enacting their previous times together and dreaming of being with him again that her whole body quivered with anticipation.

She closed her eyes and relaxed under him. Sliding her hands down his chest, her fingers found his belt. She quickly undid the belt, unbuttoned his pants and unzipped him. He groaned against her mouth as she thrust her hand under his boxer briefs to grasp his hardened shaft.

"Maybe we should slow this down," He murmured against her lips, as he slipped two fingers between her soft moist folds.

She moaned, a jolt of pleasure flowing through her. "Oh God. Oh Damon." She began to stroke him, swiping off a pearl of cum from the tip of his dick with her thumb. "I've dreamed of you so many times."

"Me too Kat," he groaned, his voice strained as he pulled his lips from hers and began to run a line of kisses down the side of her neck. He stroked her slit a couple of times and then focused on her clit, using his thumb to stroke her swollen nub while he thrust two fingers deep within her making her cry out at the sweet intrusion.

She stroked him harder, faster, as she spread her legs wider, giving him better access to her core. Ripples of pleasure raced down her spine as his fingers worked like magic, stroking her inner wall, in just the right spot to rapidly bring her to the brink.

His cock throbbed in her fist and she could tell he was coming as close as she was to climaxing.

His lips covered hers again, kissing her hard and with the passion of a man of desperation and her lips were his only salvation. His tongue thrust into her mouth, forcing her tongue into submission.

She bucked against his hand, urging his fingers deeper. Her pussy was beginning to throb, she was amazingly close. Seconds away. She became light-headed and cried out against his lips as she was overtaken by the rush of her desire. A flood of her juices greeted his probing fingers and dripped down her ass and onto his jacket.

Damon pulled his lips from hers and gazed into her eyes, the fire and tension in his eyes and expression, blaring. He kept stroking her, building her desire once more and she became swept away in a series of orgasms. Once the final tremor of her series of climaxes passed Damon removed his hand and placed a hand on either side of her head. His eyes grew darker, her desire reflected in them.

"Oh God, please come Damon. Please, come for me." She stroked him harder, faster.

"Stop or I'm going to come Kat," Damon groaned and captured her lips once more as he leaned into her.

His words only spurred her on. She needed to feel his cum, in or on her, she didn't care which as long as he gave in to her. His dick throbbed in her hand, as he prepared to release. Pulling her thin strip of wet lace aside she ran the head of his dick along her warm, moist slit and that became his undoing.

Damon pulled his lips from hers, and groaned low and feral as his cock thickened and a stream of his cum came shooting from the tip coating her mound and lower abdominals. Several more shots of his seed followed the first and the feel of his warm cum, dripping between her folds and covering her mound sent her spiralling over the edge once more.

Damon's body relaxed over hers and she released his shaft to slip her hands around his waist and hold tight to him.

"Get up!" Damon jumped back out of her embrace and took a couple steps back from her and the car.

"What?" Still reeling from her several orgasms and dripping with their combined fluids. Katrina sat up, and ran a shaky hand through her blonde locks, trying to clear the cobwebs from her mind as she watched him hurriedly do up his pants.

"Katrina! Hurry!" Taking her hand he pulled her unceremoniously from the hood of the car and tugged her skirt down. She stumbled against him, due to the combination of her heels sinking into the gravel and her slightly light-headed state.

A bright light spotlighting them made her realize the reason for his abruptness. A car was approaching and was in the process of stopping behind their car.

Awwwww shit. Their intimate time together was done. She spun around to see a police car, the driver's side door opening and a tall, thickly build officer stepping out. The headlights of the car blinded her from seeing anything more about him then his silhouette.

"So what's going on up here?" the officer asked, with a knowing tone in his voice.

Katrina cringed, feeling like a teenager caught by her parents doing something naughty. She supposed she was, but instead they were adults and it was a cop instead of their parents.

The officer stepped out of the light and Katrina let out a low sigh. Mark Glover.

"Hey Mark." Despite her relief, a tinge of embarrassment still lingered.

"Well, well, well Katrina Alexander. I haven't seen you around in a while." He turned his dark eyes over to Damon and his mouth went slack. "Holy shit! Damon Garratt." He stepped up to Damon and pulled him into a quick embrace. "Been a long time man."

"Since graduation," Damon confirmed.

Mark stepped back and gave his head a shake. "I can't believe you're back. For the reunion?"

Damon and Katrina nodded in unison.

"I'm in awe with how well you've done man," Mark continued. "I was going to go to the reunion, but we were short staffed tonight."

Katrina's eyes drifted over to Damon and saw him becoming slightly agitated. He gave Mark a tight smile and nodded. "Yeah. Not bad."

"Shit man. Not bad!" Mark turned to Katrina and jerked his thumb in Damon's direction. "Did you see the spread they had on him in..." He frowned. "*Forbes* maybe? *Time*. Dammit I can't remember. One of those. Read it while I was waiting for my daughter at the dentist office the other day."

Katrina cocked her head to the side and eyed Damon. His expression became impassive. "Really?"

"Oh yeah. They had their annual richest people in America list and he's the youngest person to have ever made that list." He looked back at Damon, awe in his expression. "Amazing man. Who'd have known. You were always a smart mother fucker, but..."

Katrina's mouth dropped open. She had no idea. She knew he'd done well, but to be one of the richest men in America! She was speechless.

"So are you two..." His grin widened, continuing to address Damon. "Back together?" He shifted his eyes back to Katrina.

Katrina glanced over at Damon and he caught her gaze.

"We're reconnecting," Damon offered. The way he said *reconnecting* sent a shiver through her. She was thankful for the darkness of the night, as she considered all the ways she'd like to *reconnect* with him, and felt the warmth colouring her cheeks. As the men caught up, in a busy banter she stood back and watched Damon. He was the same Damon, but there was so much more to him that she needed to learn.

Chapter 6

"So I was thinking..."

Katrina glanced over at Damon behind the wheel, brow raised waiting for him to continue.

"What's the chance of you getting the next week off?"

Katrina thought about her schedule. She had banquets all next week, every night, Monday to Sunday. "Horrible."

His face fell. "When do you work next?"

"Monday night."

"Can you get people to fill in?"

Katrina laughed, reached over and gave his thigh a squeeze. "Not if I want to pay the rent this month."

"What if money wasn't an issue?"

"But it is."

"What if it wasn't?" he persisted. "Could you get the week off?"

The hotel had just hired a group of new servers, so she supposed between Farrah and the new staff she could get the shifts covered. She looked over at him, catching his gaze. She knew what he was getting at. He was offering to pay her bills, but she wasn't sure how she felt about that.

"I don't want handouts Damon."

Damon huffed and gave her a look that said, *don't be stupid Katrina.*

"But-"

"Hey, when we were young, you were fine with me paying for the movie or dinner."

Katrina laughed. "Yeah, well that was cheap night at the theatre and a trip to McDonalds."

"Doesn't matter."

"Sure it does."

Not replying Damon pulled the car into the parking lot of the hotel and headed for the secure underground parking. He remained silent as he swiped his card into the card reader to raise the garage doors. Once open, he drove in and slipped the car into his assigned parking slot. Turning off the car, he turned to her, his expression serious.

"I never stopped caring for you Katrina. Even after all these years. Seeing you has reminded me of those feelings and how insane I was to allow my ambition to blind me."

Katrina opened her mouth to respond, but no sound came out. In fact, she had no idea how to respond.

"If you ever loved me then allow me a week. Allow me to try and make it up to you. Maybe I don't deserve a chance to make it up, but I'm asking. I'm a selfish, arrogant prick like that. Give this a chance to see if what we had all those years ago was as real as I remember it to be. As we both thought it was."

Katrina's eyes caught his and she saw the genuine need and yearning for her in his eyes. It wouldn't hurt right? She sighed. *I could just be setting myself up to be hurt again.* Could this just be history repeating itself?

Damon touched the side of her face and stroked her cheek with his thumb. His touch so light and intimate she closed her eyes and savoured the touch. It was so crazy, but... She slowly opened her eyes to see him still staring, waiting with baited breath for her answer.

She nodded. "Alright. I'll have my shifts covered and spend the week with you."

"Thank you Kat," Damon leaned into her and brushed his lips across hers. "Thank you."

Instead of deepening the kiss, Damon pulled back grinning like a schoolboy that had her grinning back at him. "So, have you ever been to Houston."

"I thought you said you live in New York?"

"I do," he confirmed, "But I also have a ranch in Houston."

"A ranch. With horses and stuff."

"Uh-huh."

"I love horses." She could never afford to go out horseback riding often, or get the time off to take an afternoon to go, but when she did she cherished every moment she was able to go.

"I know."

"Boy, do you ever know how to woo a girl, Damon Garratt," she teased.

"Only the ones I feel are worth wooing, Katrina Alexander."

"You own this! Oh-my-god, and it even has your *name* on it!" Katrina squealed. Her blue eyes went wide and an expression of childlike amazement appeared on her face as they approached his private plane - Garratt Enterprises was written across the side.

"Well my company owns it."

She rolled her eyes at him. "Semantics."

As they approached the door on the side opened and steps descended. The pilot stepped into the open doorway and gave them a wave. "Mr. Garratt. Miss Alexander. Good to see you both."

Damon motioned for Katrina to climb the steps before him, following behind. His eyes glanced down to her round ass in the tight faded blue jeans she was wearing. He resisted the urge to caress her ass. As much as he'd wanted to spend the night with her the previous evening he knew they had to have a serious talk before they became more intimate.

You need to tell her now, a voice in the back of his head urged. He knew he should, but couldn't get up the nerve - not yet anyhow. It was like if he didn't talk about the cancer then maybe it wouldn't be real. Irrational? Very. But he cringed at the thought of seeing her eyes fill with sympathy and sorrow when he told her. He didn't want to be pitied, or treated differently by her. But, before the chemo treatments began he'd have to tell her. Especially when in the matter of a couple of weeks he'd be bald as a baby's bottom. He'd never shaved his head before and wondered if it would suit him - he hoped so. Chicks dug bald men didn't they?

I'll know soon enough, he mused. *Besides, why ruin our time together. At least a few days. Then I'll tell her.*

They entered the plane and Damon ushered Katrina into the cabin area.

"This is gorgeous," she gushed as her eyes scanned every inch of the cabin. Damon found himself flushing slightly, not used to people having such an exuberant reaction to his plane. For most of the people that boarded with him, flying in private planes was commonplace.

"Well, thank you."

"You really have done well for yourself. This is amazing." She turned and nudged him in the side, right over the incision. Damon winced and jerked away from her.

Frowning, Katrina eyed his side, and then lifted her eyes to meet his. "I'm sorry. Are you okay? I didn't think."

Damon gritted his teeth and pushed back the urge to wince a second time. "I'm fine. Little bruised that's all."

"Oh-my-god. I'm so sorry. Let me see." She reached out to him and was about to grab at his shirt to pull it up and inspect his "bruise," but he pulled away, batting at her hands.

"I'm fine sweetie. *Really.* No big deal."

Her eyes narrowed. "You winced yesterday as well. Damon, let me see." She made an attempt to grab at his shirt again, but this time instead of fending her off, he pulled her into him. Sliding a hand into her hair and grasping the back of her head, he lowered his lips to hers and kissed her with intensity and passion - hoping to get her mind off of his side and onto other more pleasant things.

And what's going to happen when she sees you without a shirt jackass, the voice in the back of his mind nagged.

Please be seated and fasten your safely belts as we prepare for liftoff. The captain's voice announced over the speakers.

Damon pulled back and was pleased to see the desire flaring up in her eyes, his *bruise* forgotten.

"Come on." Damon led her to the set of four black leather seats facing each other and divided by a table. Once Katrina was seated, he sat across from her and secured his safety belt.

"This is really, *really* cool Damon. I feel like some sort of celebrity. I never in a million years thought I'd be in a private plane."

Damon grinned. He couldn't wait to see her expression and excitement when she set foot onto the ranch and he gave her the tour.

*****

"Can I ask you something Damon?" Katrina looked over at Damon behind the steering wheel, taking them back to his ranch.

Katrina could only imagine what his ranch looked like, maybe something straight out of the shows *Dynasty* or *Dallas*. She looked around her at the interior of the Lamborghini. Beautiful. Taking a ride in a Lamborghini, yet another first for her.

"Sure. What?"

"How many cars do you have?"

Damon chuckled. "I love cars. You know that."

"I do know, but just how much do you love them?"

Damon's grin widened. "I have two in New York and then eight at the ranch."

"And none worth less than a hundred grand either, right?" she teased. Despite her teasing, she was in awe. She couldn't even afford to get her little clunker fixed. To think Damon had enough money to buy so many lavish cars.... Wow. Her head was still spinning from it all.

"None."

"That's insane Damon."

Damon gave her a wink. "I prefer eccentric."

Katrina laughed. She watched as his hand shifted the gears, working the gears and clutch like a pro as they raced down the highway. She sat back and enjoyed the ride, the hum of the powerful engine, combined with the whoosh of his deeply threaded tires were surprisingly relaxing. Perhaps it was partly due to the beautiful man beside her - a man she never imagined she'd see again let alone be spending the next week with.

Watch yourself Katrina, don't go falling back in love with him, the voice in the back of her mind cautioned her. *I'm not even sure I fell out of love with him to begin with*, she argued. The voice fell silent.

He pulled off of the highway and onto a two lane road, trees lining both sides of the road. They travelled for roughly ten minutes before his ranch came into view. Katrina gasped, her eyes widening as they surveyed the massive two story property coming into view, beyond a twelve foot high iron gate.

Damon slowed the car to the swipe and keypad situated several feet before the gate. Reaching into his inner jacket pocket he produced a car key and lowered the window. He swiped the card into the pad and then proceeded to punch in a code. The keypad beeped three times and then the gate creaked as it slowly began to part.

"My God Damon. This house is...." She had no words. To the left of the house was a massive stable, with several horses fenced in and lounging in the pastures.

The car proceeded into the property and moments after it cleared the gate, the gate slowly closed behind them. The drive to the house took another minute or two.

"Holy shit! Is that a..." Katrina undid her seat belt and sat up straighter in her seat, eyeing the massive, powerfully build grey and white dog coming towards them. But it wasn't a dog.

"It's a grey wolf." Damon offered.

"Is it your pet?" The wolf came rushing up the car, but kept a solid three feet away from the car, running on her side, eyeing her with both interest and suspicion.

"His name is Gabe. And yes, he's my pet. I've had him since he was a pup."

Katrina shifted excitedly in the seat, anxious to jump out and touch the massive beast. "I can touch him, right?" She took her eyes from the wolf to look over at Damon.

"You can, but there are some rules I need to go over with you first."

"Okay..."

"I get out first and once he's interested in me I want you to get out and slowly, but without fear, approach us. Once you're within six feet, crouch down and don't make eye contact. Let him come to you. Once he finishing his examination of you and his body relaxes, then you can face him, pet him, hug him, whatever... No sudden movements and if he nips don't bat at him or jerk away, he'll interpret the movement as you wanting to play and sometimes he plays rough. He doesn't mean to, but he's a big boy and..." Damon shrugged. "He doesn't realize his own strength. He treats humans as he would another wolf in his pack. You'll learn."

Damon placed the car into park and promptly got out. The wolf rushed around the front of the car to greet him. Katrina waited impatiently for Damon's signal for her to get out. She was itching to stroke his long, soft fur. When Damon motioned for her to exit she had to force herself to remain calm and not rush over towards the animal. Doing as told as she rounded the car, she crouched down, keeping her eyes averted. She heard the wolf approach with suspicion. Its nose nudged her under the chin, causing her to giggle. Her giggle seemed to rile him up and he nudged her a little more roughly, nipping at her shoulder. Keeping Damon's advice in mind she didn't react even though his teeth pinched, however, she doubted it broke the skin.

"It's okay you can look at him now."

She lifted her eyes and turned, becoming eye to eye with him. Her blue eyes gazed into his stunning yellow, green ones. She slowly lifted her hands and began to stroke his fur. Seemly pleased with being petted he opened his mouth and licked her face, smack dab on the lips.

"Oh-my-god, that's so gross," Katrina squealed wiping her lips, but didn't pull away, instead she leaned into him, giving him affection in the way she would any other dog. Enjoying the attention Gabe began to get a little rowdy, nudging her and nipping lightly, followed by several licks.

"Gabe. Enough." Damon's voice boomed and made Gabe freeze and slowly back away from her, head bowed.

"He's amazing Damon," Katrina said, awe in her voice.

Damon extended his hand to her, helping her to her feet. "Well, if you liked him, then you're going to love what else is on the property."

Childlike excitement rushed through her. "What else do you have? Show me!"

Laughing Damon shook his head. "Don't you want to see the inside of the house? Your room perhaps?"

"Nope. Show me the animals. You know animals are my weakness."

Damon kept her hand in his and they began to walk along the outside of the house, Gabe trailing along behind them. "Boy do I ever remember. You got me in a lot of shit over those two dogs in the shed."

"Oh my God, I totally forgot about them. Shaggy and Scooby."

"Yeah, Shaggy and Scooby had me tossed out on my ear and put into a different foster home."

Katrina laughed. While it hadn't been funny at the time, in retrospect it was. "The Johnsons were pretty pissed weren't they?"

Damon nodded, but laughed along with her. "Oh yeah. But in their defence the dogs did chew up the seat of their new Harley. And they urinated and shit on pretty much everything stored in the shed."

"They had no place to go. We had to save them," she protested, laughing harder.

"Uh-huh."

As they rounded the corner of the building a loud roar caused Katrina to freeze in her steps. Damon tugged on her hand and she continued to follow. "Is that a..." She didn't get the words out of her mouth, because they rounded the corner and she spotted the source of the noise. A massive tiger paced behind a fenced in area.

"Holy shit!" Hearing her voice a second one emerged from the woods.

"There are two. Both females. Sasha and Sophia. They're sisters. Both rescues."

"Rescues?" She picked up the pace, nearly dragging Damon behind her.

"Yup. The Humane Society had responded to complaints of a couple having exotic pets locked in their garage. As it turns out, they'd bought the tigers as cubs from a breeder and were told they were *miniature* tigers."

"What? Miniature tigers?"

He glanced down at her, brow cocked. "These people had two six hundred pound tigers locked in a garage. They weren't the brightest of people."

"Okay, so do you go in the cage with them?" She approached the cage and the tigers came to the fence to greet her, brushing up against the chain link and flopping onto their sides. She looked up at him.

Damon laughed. "You can't go in, but feel free to pet them through the links in the cage. They're very tame, but they're too big to risk being in the same enclosure. I doubt they would intentionally hurt a human, but they're too big and powerful to risk it. One swat or playful nip to the neck and..."

Katrina was slightly disappointed, but knelt and began to stroke the big cat's head. She tickled it behind the ears and under the chin.

A ragged purr-like sound came from him, along with a low groaning.

"It's their way of purring. They can't purr like a normal small cat."

"This is so cool. But finish the story. How did you get them?"

Damon knelt beside her and began to stroke the fur of the other cat. "Well, usually I buy businesses to make money. But one of the Zoos in Houston was struggling. It was going to go bankrupt, so I stepped in and took it over."

"So it makes money now?"

Damon laughed. "No. It bleeds money. Anyhow, in the case of the wolf, one of the female wolves at the zoo had pups and I took one. In the case of the tigers, there wasn't enough space at the zoo and they were in desperate need of a place. I had the cage built for them. It spans a couple of acres. I have a permit that names the ranch an animal sanctuary and I have zookeepers come in each day to care for the animals."

"What else do you have?" Seemingly jealous of the attention the cats were getting Gabe came up to Katrina's side and bumped into her, knocking her to the ground. He proceeded to straddle her and give her another lick. Luckily she turned her head in time so his tongue lapped at her ear instead of across her lips. "Gabe!" Katrina squealed, while laughing and struggling to sit up.

"Off," Damon bellowed. Gabe immediately leapt from Katrina and sulked, its eyes downcast. Damon offered her his hand. "Come on. Let's go inside and I can give you the rest of the tour later tonight."

Katrina was slightly disappointed, wanting to see the rest of his animals, but she nodded and allowed herself to be pulled to her feet.

Chapter 7

Damon had shown Katrina to her room and then while she unpacked and made herself at home, he took the opportunity to answer some emails and check his messages. He'd called his secretary and had her postpone all of his appointments. The ones he couldn't postpone he was going to have his second in command, Kevin Gilbert, step in for him. He planned on devoting his whole week to Katrina. If things worked out as well as he expected and hoped then he's let her know about the cancer and perhaps pass by her the idea of getting married and bearing his child.

You should tell her now, just in case, the nagging voice at the back of his mind stated. He growled and pushed back his conscience on the matter. Was it too much to ask that he have one week to enjoy Katrina's company before the hammer fell, the chemo started and he had to endure the look of pity in her stunning blue eyes? He thought not.

A soft knock came at the door, causing him to lift his eyes from the paperwork he was sorting through.

"Come in."

Opening the door to his study, the maid poked her head in. "I'm about to take off for the day. Is there anything else you need before I leave Damon?"

Damon shook his head. "No. And take the rest of the week off."

"But-"

Damon raised his hand, cutting her off. "You'll be paid Lily. Katrina is here for the week and we'd like some privacy, so we'll manage."

The older lady's hazel eyes lit up, a smile touching her lips. "She's a pretty girl."

"Yes, she is."

"It's nice to see you taking some time for yourself Damon. You don't do that enough and especially with what you've been through recently..."

Lily didn't realize the cancer was still rampant within him. As far as she knew he was cured. Her husband had passed just a little over a year ago due to cancer and he just didn't want to upset or worry her. She had enough on her plate. Lily was the closest person to him in the world and if his plan to have an heir didn't pan out and he was dead within the year, his fifty-five year old widowed maid would be a very rich woman.

Damon smiled. "I'm fine Lily and you're right. I'm taking the week to myself."

"You deserve it."

"Did you set supper out in the conservatory?"

"Yes. It's out and covered. Though I would hurry if I were you. Ralph was eyeballing it pretty good."

Damon laughed. Ralph was a massive blue and red macaw. He was a bit of a potty mouth, but he was a good bird and the entertainment value he gave was priceless. "Well Lily, have a good week off."

"Have you seen Damon?" Katrina's voice asked from down the hallway.

"He's in his office dear." Lily stepped back out into the hallway, to address Katrina.

Damon's ears perked up and his smile widened as he heard Katrina's voice from out in the hallway. "I'm in here Kat."

Lily and Damon's eyes locked and she gave him a knowing nod of the head. "Have a good week Damon."

"You too, Lily."

Lily disappeared and was replaced by Katrina. She'd changed out of the jeans and t-shirt and was now wearing a simple yellow spaghetti strap sundress. The bodice hugged her modest breasts and the skirt fell to just above the knees. Her hair was pulled up into a high ponytail that swung back and forth behind her head. She looked as fresh and beautiful as she had when they were young. It was like the clock had turned back, and he was sitting before the woman he'd left, possibly making the biggest mistake of his life.

"What?" She shifted uncomfortably from foot to foot, a flush heating up her cheeks. "You're looking at me kinda...."

Damon laughed as he stood. "I was thinking that you haven't aged a day since high school."

Katrina laughed with him, but lowered her eyes to the floor, her blush deepening. "I guarantee the cellulite on my ass and thighs would disagree."

Walking around the desk, his eyes lowered to her calves, her thighs hidden by the skirt. "From what I can see, your legs are incredible. But if you want to remove the dress I can give you a more thorough examination." He gave her a wink and she rolled her eyes at him.

"Your house is beautiful," she commented meeting his eyes and changing the subject.

"You went exploring?"

She chewed at her lower lip, her embarrassment evident in her eyes." I kinda got lost trying to find your office."

Taking her hand, he gave it a tug. "Come on, there's a part of the house I'm sure you haven't seen yet. And our supper is sitting in it, waiting for us." He couldn't believe he was so excited to show her the conservatory or the adjoining aquarium. She'd been so excited to see the other animals, he knew she'd be beside herself when she saw the aquarium and met Ralph.

"Oh? Maybe I have."

Glancing down at her, Damon smiled. "Oh, if you had, then you wouldn't be near as calm as you are right now."

*****

Damon's whole ranch was one big surprise after another. She absolutely adored it, but certainly wasn't what she'd expected. Maybe his place in New York was different, but aside from the size of the house, the cars in the garage, and the exotic animals living on the premises, the house reminded her of an average home. Abet a home of a wealthy person, but not one that was worth billions. It really made her curious about his New York home.

The thought of how it wasn't lavish quickly left her mind as he led her into a tunnel that led to the conservatory. The tunnel was roughly twenty feet long and it was actually a large salt water aquarium. Thousands of colourful fish swam to the left, right and above them.

She stopped dead in her tracks halfway through the tunnel and stepped up to the curved glass. "Oh-my-God, Damon! This is incredible!" Being surrounded by the water and fish was nothing short of incredible. It was a set-up she'd expect to see in a large public aquarium, not in a private home. But then again, nothing in this home was typical.

Damon chuckled as he stepped up behind her and slid his arms around her waist. She sighed and fell back into him. She savoured the feel of his arms surrounding her as her eyes followed the assortment of fish racing back and forth. She could easily stand there for hours just watching them swim around her. It was calming. It was perfect.

"How long did this take to build?"

"Few months. There's a company that does custom aquariums based out of LA. I had them come down and build it."

"It's breathtaking. I don't think I've seen anything like it. There's no words. Is your place in New York like this one?"

"Nope. It's more traditional." Damon leaned down and kissed the side of her neck, sending a shiver through her. She pressed back into him, placing her hands over his.

"It's such an amazing house. It feels like I've stepped into another world. I swear I could live here the rest of my life and be perfectly happy."

"Really?"

The seriousness in his tone had her pulling her eyes from the fish and over her shoulder to look at him. "Who wouldn't; it's paradise."

Damon laughed and lowered his lips to hers. He kissed her softly and pulled away, leaving her longing for a longer, deeper kiss.

"Then wait until you see what I have to show you next."

"I don't think I can handle many more surprises."

He stepped back from her and motioned for her to follow him. Katrina hesitated a moment as she admired his broad shoulders under the grey form-fitting long-sleeved turtleneck shirt he was wearing, and as her eyes lowered, his ass caught her attention - hard and muscular under his jeans.

Her mind raced back to the previous evening when he'd brought her to orgasm with his fingers. How good would his tongue feel between her legs? His cock? She'd experienced it before, but it had been a long time and he'd been her first. She'd always considered him the best she'd ever had - in all ways, but it had been so long the memories had faded slightly - the lines were blurred between what she remembered and what she made up in her head when she pleasured herself thinking of him. And since there had been so many years past since they'd last been together, perhaps he had even more tricks up his sleeve?

She longed to find out.

"Well, come on." Damon glanced over his shoulder and motioned for her to catch up.

As she came closer to the glass doors at the end of the aquarium tunnel she began to hear chirping.

Opening the door Damon ushered her in. "Hustle or they'll get out and we'll spend the evening chasing them though the house."

Katrina moved as fast as her heels would let her and brushed past him and into yet another spectacular room. The room was a gigantic conservatory and most of the birds appeared to be behind a thin metal mesh. However, her eyes immediately spotted a massive parrot sitting at the center of a round white table. He was focused on trying to pry the lid off a large silver platter.

As they approached the parrot lifted his head and froze his beak on the handle of the lid. He eyed her, then Damon and then back to her. He released the lid and took a step back, lowering his head as if upset that he was caught.

"Wasn't me," he squawked.

Katrina bit down on her lower lip, as she watched him pull himself up to his full height. "Wasn't me," he repeated, followed by, "fucker." He began to shift from foot to foot, flapping his wings as if daring them to challenge him.

Katrina's mouth dropped open, shocked for a moment before a burst of laughter erupted from her. She glanced over at Damon who was also grinning, but didn't seem near as shocked as she was at Ralph's explicit language.

Damon put his arm out and whistled. Ralph immediately took flight and landed on Damon's arm. Damon reached into his front pants pocket and pulled out a mini carrot passing it to Ralph. Grabbing it with his left foot, Ralph eyed Katrina as he chewed at the carrot. Once he was done he began getting anxious, rocking back and forth, his eyes glued to Katrina who had come to stand beside Damon.

"Hello," he cooed, his head rocking back and forth.

Katrina smiled and looked at Damon, catching his smiling eyes.

"Hello... Hello... Hello.... HELLLLOOOO!" He screeched flapping his wings to gain their attention.

Damon laughed. "For God sakes say hi before Ralph takes a heart attack. He doesn't like being ignored."

Still smiling, Katrina turned her attention back to Ralph. "Hello Ralph."

Ralph stopped his rocking and seemingly satisfied with the introductions, spread his wings and flew over to a perch by the table a few feet away.

"Is he a rescue as well?" Katrina asked as they made their way to the little table.

"Nope. I've had him since he was old enough to be taken from the breeder. He usually goes wherever I go. He's been all over the US and has his own room in the house in Manhattan." Damon pulled out a chair for her, motioning for to sit. "He's as close to family as I have," he shrugged, "aside from the housekeeper Lily."

Chapter 8

There it was - the look of pity in her eyes. He hated that look. She used to get that same look each time he was thrown into a new foster home. He regretted his previous statement. She had a way of making him say things without filter - not something he generally did. Usually, every word, every move, every action was calculated.

Damon turned and took a seat across from her, busying himself with opening the stainless steel container.

"Mom said if you don't drop by and say hi when we get back to Bangor, you'll be in big trouble bucko. Her exact words."

Damon grinned and released a sigh of relief at the change in topic. Lifting the cover he uncovered a BBQ rotisserie chicken with a number of pasta salads and potato wedges. One of her favourite meals - or used to be anyhow.

"How are your parents anyhow?" He couldn't believe he hadn't even asked of them.

"Divorced." She replied grabbing a potato wedge and popping it into her mouth. "This smells delicious, by the way."

"I'll forward the compliment to Lily." He opened a bottle of wine and began to pour some, while she helped herself to the chicken. "What happened there?" Not that he was shocked; he could see a divorce in their future even when they were kids. All her parents ever did was fight.

"Dad decided to marry his secretary and mom has sworn off of men, apparently you are all swine that can't be trusted." She said matter-of-factly, an amused gleam in her eyes.

Damon lifted a brow at her. "That a fact? And she wants me to drop in and say hi?"

Katrina grinned. "Go figure huh? She always liked ya."

"And your dad is with the secretary?"

Katrina scooped up a spoonful of macaroni salad and grinned. "Pretty cliché, huh?"

"Indeed."

"Have you ever had a thing for your secretary?"

Damon paused, his glass of wine partway to his mouth. His mind raced backward in time two years when he'd first hired Becky.

"Oh-my-God! You dog, you did!" Grabbing a potato wedge, Katrina tossed it at him, hitting him square in the chest. "That's so nasty!"

"'I didn't say that!" he defended, blocking another potato wedge that came sailing across the table at him.

"You don't have to. I can see it written all over your face. You're the worst liar ever, Damon Garratt!" Despite her mock outrage, he could see the humour in her eyes.

Damon set his glass down and spread his arms out, palms out in mock surrender. "Okay, okay it happened once. At the office."

Her eyes widened and a wide smile spread across her lips. "Not on your desk!"

He could feel his face grow hot. "Not here. But in New York, in the actual office... Yes. Once." He felt the need to seriously stress *once.*

She cocked her head to the side and eyed him, clucking her tongue off the roof of her mouth. "So once, huh?"

He nodded.

"But you never brought her here?"

His smile faded and he reached across the table to take her hands in his, partly because he wanted to touch her and partly because he wanted to ensure he didn't get another potato wedge chucked at him. "I never bring anyone here Katrina."

Her smile faded as her gaze caught his. "Never."

He shook his head. "I've had the ranch five years and you're the first I've brought here." He gave her hand a tug and she stood and made her way around the table to perch herself on him, straddling his lap, her skirt riding all the way up her thighs.

Damon pulled her tight and brushed his lips along the side of her neck. The sweet smell of apples washed over him. She smelt so good. She *felt* so good. How in the name of God had he been able to leave her? She sighed softly and let her head drop to the side, giving him better access to the tender flesh.

"Why haven't you brought anyone here?"

"Just haven't." Damon nipped at the side of her neck and she gasped, her fingers fisting his shirt at the shoulders. He ran his tongue along the side and up to her earlobe, nipping lightly.

"No. I... Why me?"

"I think you know," he murmured. She wiggled on his lap bringing his dick to life. It swelled as his hand slipped up her outer thigh and caressed her bare ass. Bare? The little vixen wasn't wearing any panties. His dick went from semi-hard to rock solid in two seconds flat at the discovery.

"This is crazy Damon," she gasped, as he began to kiss his way across her jaw to her lips.

"Crazy is the fact that you didn't put on panties Miss Alexander," he chided, and then claimed her mouth before she had a chance to respond.

Her lips parted for him in a soft moan that rocked him to the core with need. His tongue thrust into her mouth, which tasted of sweet wine to duel with hers. The ache in his dick increased and he had to fight to keep his desire reigned in. He couldn't remember wanting her - or anyone for that matter - so badly. How he was going to be able to hold back from taking her until they had "the" discussion he had no clue.

She pulled back from him, pressing her forehead to his, her breathing ragged. "I ummm." She closed her eyes and buried her face against his neck. Her body trembled over his.

"Hmmm. Kat."

She pulled back and caught his eyes, the desire flaring in her eyes. "Would you believe me if I said I forgot to pack them?"

Damon threw back his head as a roar of laughter rocked through him. "Not for a second."

A loud crash sounded behind Katrina, keeping him from responding. They both turned to see Ralph had snuck onto the table and was standing on the chicken, his beak covered in macaroni salad and in the middle of eating a potato wedge. Sensing he was being watched Ralph lifted his eyes and looked from Damon to Katrina and back again.

"Wasn't me," Ralph squawked, despite being caught red-handed. "Fuckers!"

Katrina giggled and her face lit up with amusement. "I think dinner is ruined."

"We can go to the kitchen and get something else, or I can take you out to eat." Damon glanced down at his watch. 7pm. "The night is still young."

Katrina brushed her lips across his. "The last thing I want to do is leave. Not when we're comfortable. And..." She kissed her way to his neck.

Damon's body tensed. Maybe he should just lay it all on the line now and then... No. Not yet. "Hey, I have an idea..." He stood, and she slid from his lap to stand in front of him.

*****

Katrina groaned inwardly. *What does a girl have to do to get some more action with this man?* It was sweet that he didn't want to rush things - but damn! Every part of her wanted him. She'd never thrown herself on a man like this before. It was evident he wanted her as much as she wanted him, so what was the problem? Sure they hadn't seen each other for a decade, but they were hardly strangers.

"We can drop this in the kitchen and then figure something out." Damon called over his shoulder at her. Carrying the wine, Katrina followed Damon out of the conservatory, through the aquarium tunnel and into the house.

"I'm really not hungry anyhow Damon. I gorged on the plane remember?"

"Well, if you're sure. It just occurred to me that since I gave Lily the week of we'll have to fend for ourselves. I hope you can cook because-"

"- you still suck at it," she finished for him, quickening her pace so she was walking at his side.

He looked down at her and cocked a brow, amused. "You know how much I hate when you do that."

"Finish your-"

"-sentences," he interrupted. "Yes."

"Smart ass," she grumbled, rolling her eyes and fighting a grin threatening to emerge. "First off, you let Lily have the week off?"

"Yeah, thought we could have some privacy." He gave her a wink that sent a shiver through her. Mixed signals or what!

She was about to respond when they reached the kitchen. For at least the hundredth time since she entered the house she was speechless. The kitchen was massive, equipped with the latest and newest appliances. Glancing at the stove, it looked more like the control panel to launch a NASA space shuttle then a stove. Maybe they would be eating out.

She ran her fingers along the marble countertops. "This is incredible Damon. I think my entire apartment would fit into this kitchen."

Damon's eyes scanned the room and he nodded. "I like it." Grabbing a bucket from under the sink he tossed it all in.

"What are you doing?"

"Gabe will love this. He'll have it gone within a minute. Waste not, want not and all that; especially when you have some housemates with some seriously large appetites."

"He'll eat macaroni salad?"

"Oh yeah, mixed with rotisserie chicken. Hell yeah."

"And as I think about it, it's beautiful out tonight, so there's another area of the house I'd like to show you."

"Do you have flamingos in the back yard Damon?" From what she's seen so far it wouldn't have surprised her.

Damon smirked. "Not yet."

"An elephant?"

Damon laughed outright. "No. Actually, you've seen all of the animals, aside from the horses that I'm sure you noticed as we drove in."

"Then what?" She was dying with suspense. It appeared that with Damon anything was possible.

Hooking his index finger under her chin, he lifted her eyes to his, leaned down and kissed her softly. "Patience, Kat." Lifting the bucket he exited motioning for her to follow him. "Bring the wine."

*****

As suspected it was late enough in the evening that the sun had almost completely fallen behind the mountain range, leaving red and orange streaks in the darkened sky. Damon dumped the dinner into Gabe's dish that Gabe immediately began to gobble down - barely taking time to swallow - as if he hadn't been fed in a week, when in all actuality he'd been fed that afternoon.

Damon loved how she was beaming from ear to ear. Her excitement was contagious, even though he knew where he was leading them. He was beginning to feel more carefree than he had in a long, long time. Since high school if he were to be honest with himself.

The rush of gaining a new business and seeing the amounts in his bank accounts rise on a daily basis was an addictive adrenaline rush, but it wasn't true happiness. It was like an addict, waiting for his next high. The anticipation and rush were exhilarating when they got their fix, but it wasn't fulfilling. But after a while, you begin to live for the rush and only the rush and simply enjoying life becomes a forgotten desire.

With her, he was actually feeling happy. It was different than the rush he'd been living his life chasing after, it was better. It was squeezing out his need for the rush. But with it came a major drawback; the reality of how lonely and one-dimensional his life had become was like a slug to the gut. He wasted so many years chasing his next high... If the cancer hadn't put his life in limbo how many more years would he have wasted? If there was one good thing to come out of this whole ordeal then it was that he was shown what was really important in life, before he became too old to make changes. He could begin to lead a life of fulfillment instead of one consumed with his need for money and power.

Katrina slid her arm around his waist and pulled herself tight to him. Looking down at Katrina, his smile widened as their eyes locked. Draping his arm around her shoulders he pulled her just a bit tighter to his left side.

He was fighting with himself. He wanted her - badly. He was thankful for Ralph and his interruption of them earlier, because if it hadn't been for him breaking the mood, Damon wouldn't have had the power to deny her.

"Holy shit!" Katrina pulled away from his embrace as they rounded the corner and they stepped into the pool area. The pool area had been set up to look like a tiki island getaway, with a lagoon pool with waterfall and bar island in the center. Off of the pool was a hot tub.

"Hold on." Damon walked over to the control panel and opened it. Pressing a few buttons the area came alive. Tiki torches lit up surrounding the pool and soft sultry music began playing softly.

"Look at the lights in the pool!"

Damon watched, amused, as she hurried over to the pool. The soft, warm wind picked up and a gust of wind lifted her skirt giving him a view of her bare bottom, giving him his very own extremely arousing *Marilyn Monroe* style flash. He gritted his teeth, pushing down his arousal.

Damon made his way over to her, and looked down into the pool. Lights in blue, red and yellow softly shone up through the water, breaking through, moving and dancing.

She spun around to turn to him and chewed at her lower lip as she reached behind her. "But I don't have a swimsuit..." A soft unzipping sound reached his ears as the bodice of her sundress began to loosen around her.

He closed his eyes and tried to control the jerking of his dick as it came alive. "Well, we could just-"

"-Moonbath," she teased. His eyes lifted to the sky and discovered she was right, the sun was fully down and the full moon had begun to appear. She kicked off her shoes.

Touching her shoulders he slipped the straps of the dress down her upper arms. The pale yellow bodice peeled away to reveal her modest breasts that looked as beautiful to him as they had a decade ago. The dress slowly slid down her body leaving her gloriously naked for him to feast his eyes upon.

"You're stunning Kat." He could hear the admiration in his voice, apparently so did she, her cheeks coloured an alluring crimson in the moonlight. He reached out to touch her cheek, but she stepped back, turned and dove into the water. She surfaced by the pool bar, hoisting her up and onto the platform.

"Coming?" She called out to him, thirty feet away.

Kicking off his shoes he was about to pull his shirt up and over his head when the scar stopped him. Looking around he felt confident that if he stayed in the water, in the dim lighting she wouldn't notice. If she did then he could brush it off - maybe. Worse comes to worst he told he the truth much earlier than planned, but spending the week with her and not allowing himself the pleasure of her body was going to be more than he could handle.

To hell with it. Damon pulled his shirt up and over his head tossing it to the floor, his pants and underwear coming quickly after it, until he was naked with a pile of clothing at his feet. Damon glanced down at the four-inch incision on his right side. Not *too* noticeable.

"Damn. You *have* been working out!" Damon's eyes lifted to see Katrina reclined back against the tiki bar with a wine cooler in one hand the other hand waving a beer at him.

A sheepish grin touched his lips. "I try to make it to the gym from time to time." She looked stunning, her golden hair cascading down her back and her breasts begging for his touch. The water glistened under the moonlight as it flowed down the curves of her body. His jaw clenched, scared he would embarrass himself and get a full on boner like some teenager just by looking at her.

"You know... You're like the old Damon, but the 2.0 deluxe version."

Chuckling, Damon raised a brow up at her. "Never been called that before." Her eyes began to roam his body, wandering up his thighs to pause at his semi-erect dick. Not wanting her to focus on his torso, Damon dove into the water and began to swim towards hers.

As he reached the bar, he emerged from the water, but didn't pull himself up onto the landing. Instead, he crossed his arms over the side and accepted her offered beer. Opening the top he placed the cap beside him and took a long drink.

"Come on up." She patted the empty spot beside her. "I want to examine that body of yours a little closer."

That's what I'm afraid of. "I'm fine."

She grinned and chuckled softly. "Are you becoming shy or something? I've already seen ya." She motioned towards herself, "and if you hadn't noticed I'm not exactly clothed."

He let his eyes stroll their way over her body, admiring her. His dick went from semi-hard to rock solid by the time his dark eyes met her blue ones, a brow cocked at her. "Oh, believe me. I've noticed. I never remembered you being such a little exhibitionist."

She groaned loudly. "And you call *me* a princess." She placed her wine cooler beside her and leapt into the water.

Still holding onto the platform, Damon pushed back slightly and looked around him trying to see her under the water. A hand touched his calf, then thigh. Her other hand grasped his cock and stroked him several times before releasing him, making him suck in his breath through clenched teeth, his body tensing. She broke the surface of the water in front of him, placing herself between him and the platform.

She brushed her wet hair out of her face and wiped the excess water from her face, taking a deep breath in. Her make-up had run slightly leaving streaks of black under her eyes and cheeks, he was surprised at how sexy it looked, like a woman who'd been thoroughly fucked. Face grew deathly serious as she caught his eyes. "Can I ask you something Damon?"

Ahhh fuck. The scar. She must have seen it. His expression darkened. *Might as well get it over with.* A part of him was actually relieved; at least it was going to be out in the open.

Chapter 9

She wasn't used to being so brazen, but this was Damon so to hell with it. If she couldn't be comfortable enough to be herself, say what she felt, and ask for what she wanted from him then when could she? Right?

She slipped her arms around his neck, pressing her body tight to him, and using his body to keep her afloat and upright. "So what does a girl have to do to get some action around here?"

Damon's mouth dropped for a moment; snapping it shut, a grin tugged at the corners of his lips and she felt his rock hard erection jerking against her stomach. He cocked a brow at her, giving her that sexy grin of his that made her heart thump frantically in her chest.

"Now, what would you mean by *action,* Miss Alexander?"

What a bugger. He's going to make me beg.

She grazed her lips across his. "I mean, I've been throwing myself at you all day and you keep brushing me off."

"In my defence, the last time was Ralph's fault."

Katrina fought back the urge to laugh. Instead, she sighed and brushed her lips along the side of his neck and was delighted to feel him tremble against her. "But Ralph isn't here now."

He groaned softly, his body tensing against hers. "No, he's not."

Once she reached his collarbone, she ran a string of butterfly kisses back up his neck, across his jaw and to his lips again. She lifted her eyes back up to meet his and kissed his lips softly once more. "So what do I have to do?" She pressed tighter to him, her breasts crushing against his thick, sculpted chest.

He growled, low in the back of his throat. "What you're doing now might work."

She slipped one of her hands between them and grasped his thick shaft. She began to slowly stroke him.

"Th-that, I.... Ya that might work too."

"Might?" she ran her tongue along his lower lip, before gently nipping at it. "What will push you over the edge?"

"I'm trying hard to hold off, build the tension," he groaned as she tightened her grip on his dick and began to stroke a little harder.

"Oh, I think there's enough tension." Her pussy felt like it was on fire, she'd never wanted anyone so damned bad. If he wanted tension, then he'd done a damned good job at building it, and it was appearing that she'd finally begun to break through.

"If you keep doing that I'll end up blowing it here and kill the chance for action."

Releasing his cock, she grinned and slipped out from under his arm. Swimming backwards, she watched him as he turned to face her, anguish in his expression. Oh, she'd totally gotten to him. He closed his eyes, and when they reopened the fire and feral hunger had her pussy clenching in anticipation.

He lunged and began to swim towards her. Letting out a yelp, she flipped to her stomach and began to swim in earnest, her strokes hard and propelling her body quickly through the water. She could sense him approaching, but didn't look back to verify, wanting to make it to the edge before he caught up to her.

Got it! A sense of triumph washed over her as she reached the edge before him and pulled herself up and onto it, which shocked her. Damon had always been a star swimmer; it wasn't like him to be weak swimmer. However, she'd only beat him by a hair. She'd just rolled onto her back, spread eagle on the cool tile, panting wildly when he reached the side and pulled himself up. She watched his face and frowned, seeing him grimace as he pulled his stunning body from the water.

"You okay?"

He laughed lightly, and nodded. "Yeah, of course." Before she could question him further, his body was covering hers, his mouth crashing down upon hers, with the hunger and need that she'd been longing for him to kiss her with since the dance.

The warm breeze tightened her wet nipples into hardened peaks. Her body relaxed under his, as she wrapped her arms around his neck and she parted her lips, giving in to his probing tongue.

Now this was more like it.

The tile was hard under her back, as he gently lowered his body to hers. His erect shaft slipping between her legs and probed at her entrance, but the discomfort of the tile under her was nothing compared to the inferno that had flared up within her. Wrapping her legs around his waist, she pulled him down, hoping to impale herself on him, but it was a useless effort.

He pulled his lips from hers chuckling softly. Bracing a hand on either side of her head he stared down at her, humour mixed with the hunger in his gaze.

She let out an exasperated sigh. "Damon, stop being cruel!"

His chuckling got louder, throatier. "We have all night Kat." He lowered his mouth to the side of her neck and nipped. A shot of pleasure shimmed down her spine and she writhed under him, clawing at his shoulders.

She growled softly. "All night means we can do it two, three, half-dozen times."

Damon chuckled again as his mouth continued its journey along her collarbone and then down her chest. His lips rested in the valley between her breasts. "Baby, a half dozen times? You're going to kill me."

She moaned as he captured one nipple between his teeth, his tongue flicking as his teeth gently nibbled. She yelped and moaned wiggling against him. As his mouth released the first nipple and captured the second, his hand slipped between them to cup her mound.

"It would be a wonderful way to die," she gasped as he nipped a little harder and sent a delicious shiver of pleasure and pain through her. He spread her velvety folds and thrust a finger deep into her core as his tongue and teeth teased. It was good, but not enough. She clawed at his shoulders, and bucked against his hand.

"Damon please!"

"Oh, I love how you beg me," he murmured, releasing her breast and slowly moving his lips lower, down her torso and to her stomach. With each inch his mouth got closer to the apex between her legs the more intense the throbbing between her legs became and demanding her body for his became. Just when his mouth reached her mound, he stopped and stood.

"Come on."

Slowly opening her eyes, she looked at him frowning. Letting out a low, rugged breath she accept the hand he was extending to her. "So cruel," she grumbled as she allowed herself to be pulled to her feet.

As soon as she was on her feet, he pulled her into his arms and lowered his mouth to hers. Again, she was swept up in the power of his embrace and the force of his lips on hers. Her mind became a blank as the need and yearning flowed through her. She was so wrapped up in the feel and taste of him that she didn't even notice that he'd been backing her up until the back of her legs bumped into something.

Katrina yelped, tearing her lips from his as she started to topple backwards unto the double-sized wicker longer chair. His arms caught her and set her down gently onto the lounger. Damon stretched out next to her and traced the line of her jaw with his index finger, so tenderly that she could barely feel it.

His expression darkened, a frown crossing his strikingly handsome features. "We need to have a talk, Kat, before this goes any further."

Katrina mimicked his frown with one of her own. She didn't like the seriousness of his expression. She laughed lightly, running her index finger along his collarbone and that's when her eyes spotted the scar on his right side. Her soft smile faded as she sat up and pushed his arm that was partially covering the scar away to get a closer look. It was fresh.

"Were you in an accident?" As she asked the question she knew that wasn't the case. The incision was too perfect, too clean. He'd had surgery.

"No."

She fingered the scar. *Jesus, no wonder he cringed each time I nudged him in he side.* She looked back up to meet his eyes, but she couldn't read him. "What's going on Damon? That scar. That's..." Her frowned deepened. "That scar is over your lung. My God, what's going on?" She had no idea why, but she felt tears welling up in her eyes. A sinking feeling overtook her, rocking her to the core. She almost didn't want to hear what he was going to tell her because - deep down - she knew it wasn't good, she could feel it.

****

Way to kill a mood, he chastised himself. Seeing her face fall into such an intense expression of concern and seeing the tears form in her eyes was tearing him apart. A part of him wished he hadn't brought it up yet, but another wished he'd mentioned it the previous evening before she even came to Houston.

Flipping over to his back, Damon urged her to cuddle against him. She snuggled tight pressing her face against his neck. "Please Damon, tell me. What's going on?"

Damon swallowed down the lump forming in his throat. Thrusting his fingers into her hair, he slowly stoked her long, silken locks, watching the strands slowly fall one by one. She closed her eyes, savouring the delicious pull of the strands. Stroking her hair began to relax him, making it easier to say what needed to be said, although he was still deciding on how much of his plan he wanted to share - just yet.

"I had surgery."

She slowly opened her eyes. "I figured as much."

"Well, it was my lung I had a lower lobectomy."

Her brow creased. "Cancer?"

Damon nodded.

"You had lung cancer?" Disbelief was etched in her expression as she looked up at him. "But you're only twenty-nine. And you don't smoke. How..."

Damon shrugged. "I've been asking myself that very question. But they did the surgery-"

"And you're cured." she finished for him, the hope creeping into her blue eyes.

"What did I tell you about finishing my sentences Miss Alexander?" he chastised.

She grinned sheepishly and shrugged.

"I'm not cured."

Her grin faded and the tears began to well back up in her eyes. "I... But you're going to be okay, right? I mean... You'll be fine." A single tear slipped down her cheek. He brushed it away with his thumb.

"I don't know. I start chemo next week. Then radiation. I like to think that it's going to turn out okay."

She opened her mouth to speak and then snapped it shut. Instead, she lowered her face to his shoulder and tightened her grip on his waist. While her sobs were silent, he could feel the tears dripping onto his shoulder. Damn, he wished he hadn't put this on her, but she needed to know. He knew it would have been impossible to keep it from her the entire week.

****

Of all the things he could have told her, the last thing Katrina would have expected to hear was that Damon had cancer and could be dying. The last thing. It seemed so surreal. One minute they were having a great day and the next she was feeling more helpless then ever in her lifetime.

"Is that why you came to find me?"

Damon nodded. "Yes. I needed to see you."

Katrina touched the side of his face, feeling the light stubble beginning to form. "I'm glad you did." She forced herself to smile, but it was hard when all she wanted to do was bury her face against his neck and sob. But she couldn't. She couldn't imagine what he was going through; the last thing she wanted was to make him feel worse.

"I've been doing a lot of thinking."

"And..." *Where's this going?* She shifted on him, crossing her arms over his chest and resting her chin on her arms, eyeing him intently.

"Everything I worked for-" He waved at their surroundings with surprising detachment. "-It gave me a rush to obtain it all. And I thought I was happy, but when I found out the cancer wasn't gone I did some serious thinking. I've realized that I've never been happy, not since the day I left to go to California."

Katrina didn't know what to say, so she remained silent allowing him too finish speaking what was on his mind.

"I hoped and prayed you'd be single when I went to that reunion." He gave her a soft smile. "I never stopped loving you Kat. I know it's only been a day, but time *may* not be on my side so I want to make the most of it... Just in case."

She felt the tears threatening to escape once more, as she was reminded of the direness of the situation.

"Please don't honey. It's going to be okay." He took her hands and laced his fingers into hers. "I feel it. I really do." An unsure expression touched his features sparking her curiosity. There was more he wasn't saying. She could actually see him mulling something over in his head and she needed to know what it was.

"Damon. Please. Whatever is on your mind, tell me. Don't close up now."

Chapter 10

Damon commenced raking his fingers through her hair. She closed her eyes and savoured the feel. How many times, when they were young, had they spread one of those old, itchy, green army blankets out on the grass and laid side by side, looking up at the stars as he stroked and played with her hair? Countless. Something about the intimate act soothed her. Always had.

A cool breeze past over them and she shivered involuntarily. Damon paused, frowning. "Shit, I'm sorry Kat. It's getting cold and we're-" He looked down at them naked and embracing. "-pretty exposed."

"I'm okay." She wanted to hear the rest of what he had to say, she feared that moving would keep him from completely opening up to her. Despite her words, goosebumps were beginning to form on her arms and legs and she shivered a second time.

Cocking a brow up at her, Damon shot a look at her that said he didn't think so. Sliding out from under her, he stood and extended his hand to her. "Come on. We'll have some champagne by the fireplace in the den.

"Should you be drinking?" she asked, accepting his hand and getting to her feet. Damon snorted and rolled his eyes at her, but that was her only response to that question.

Not bothering to pick up their clothing, Damon took her into the part of his house which led to the den through the French double doors. Closing the door securely behind them, Damon flicked a couple switches and the fireplace lit up and the lights dimmed to a soft, yellow glow.

Grabbing a soft white blanket from over the back of an antique rocker by the French doors, he draped it over her shoulders and then made his way over to the large, mahogany antiqued bar. Perching herself on the arm of one of the leather sofas, Katrina watched his beautiful body as he walked away.

The familiar stirring between her legs flared up and a shiver of anticipation rushed down her spine. She couldn't keep her eyes off of him; his body was a masterpiece of lean muscle and definition, even with the angry scar on his right side. He popped the cork of a bottle of champagne that began to spill over onto the bar in front of him and lightly sprayed his bare chest.

"Ahh shit," he grumbled, grabbing a rag and wiping up his mess. Her giggling got his attention and he looked up, met her gaze and gave her a lopsided smile. "I should know by now that's going to happen."

Katrina's smile widened. "Live and learn baby."

His smile widened as he poured them both a glass of champagne and then made his way over to her. "Come on," he nodded towards a large cream coloured shag rug in front of the fireplace. "Grab a couple of pillows and let's relax. Then we can talk."

She let out a loud sigh of relief. He was going to tell her whatever else he had on his mind. This was good, very good.

Grabbing a couple of silk throw pillows from the sofa she'd been perched upon she walked over to the rug that he was already stretched out on and sat down. She couldn't help but let her eyes wander down the length of his body to his groin. His cock was at half-mast as it wasn't sure if action was going to take place or not, but wanted to be prepared - just in case.

"My eyes are up here missy."

Katrina groaned, rolling her eyes at him. "Just returning the favour, for all that ogling you were doing earlier."

"I don't ogle," he defended.

"No, I suppose not. It was more like leering really."

He groaned. "I don't leer."

Smiling she stretched out on her side, facing him, hugging the pillow and setting her chin upon it.

"Here." Damon passed her a glass. She took a tentative sip. The sweet liquid was just what she needed and took a deeper drink.

She watched Damon drink close to half of the glass in one swallow. She was no doctor, but she really didn't think he should be drinking especially since he was starting chemo treatments the following week, but she didn't say something. He was a big boy, it was his decision, but it still made her uneasy. She fought to keep a frown from showing in her expression. She imagined he needed it now anyhow, he was going through a lot, so who was she to tell him what to do or nag if she didn't agree.

"As I said, there's more," he began.

Katrina nodded, placing her glass on the end table next to them and then settling back down beside him. He placed his glass beside her and mimicked her position on his side facing her.

"You know I have no family."

Katrina frowned and nodded. It had been such a sad situation for him growing up. Most of the foster homes he'd lived in only had him there for the extra money from the government. The only decent family he'd been placed in was the one where she'd had talked him into taking the dogs, and well, that didn't last long - because of her. When he was eighteen he began living on his own, working at the local gas station pumping gas in the evenings after school and on weekends for a few months before heading off to California.

He swallowed hard, making her even more curious as to what he was about to get at. It was unlike him to have such a hard time broaching a topic. He took a deep breath in and released it slowly.

"Well, after we had our talk by the fountain. You know, when you mentioned you were disappointed over how things have developed for you; that you'd wished that you had children and a husband by now..."

Katrina's body froze. It was beginning to sink in what he was getting at, even though he hadn't said the words yet.

"I don't want what I've worked so hard for to be for nothing Katrina."

God dammit! The tears began to fill in her eyes again. She wished she could control her emotions, at least until he got through what he wanted to say, but it was impossible. He was throwing so much at her, so fast. It was hard. He was preparing for the worst and she didn't want to think about the worst, not with Damon, not so soon after reconnecting.

He sighed. "I'm just going to say it. It isn't romantic like I'd envisioned, but..." He thrust an agitated hand through his hair. "I'd like you to consider marrying me and us having a child."

Her mouth dropped, her eyes widening in surprise. He was serious. He was really, really serious. She'd thought he was hinting towards it, or something of the sort, but to have him actually say it out load, made it real.

"I... Ummm."

He gave his head a shake and forced a smile onto his lips. "It was a crazy idea. I'm sorry I brought it up."

Marrying Damon? Having his baby? She'd thought about it when they were younger and over the years there were many times that she'd wondered 'what if.' Was it that crazy of an idea? She didn't know. The look of disappointment in his eyes tore at her.

"Aren't you scared that I'll take you to the cleaners? And what if it turns out okay, which I'm sure it will. Then you're stuck with a wife and a child in your life."

His eyes brightened and a smile tugged at the corners of his lips. He grazed his knuckles across her cheeks and he leaned down and ghosted his lips across hers. "You wouldn't. And I couldn't think of anything better than being *stuck* with you and our baby in my life."

She smiled and leaned into him, grazing her lips along the length of his neck. He groaned softly and her smile widened. A lifetime with Damon. It was crazy and it was so fast that it had her head spinning with emotions.

He pulled back from her, to look into her eyes. "I know this is quick and insane, but I may not have the luxury of time Kat. That's the reality of the situation even though I hate to think of it. I love you Kat, I always have. If you marry me and if we have a child, you have no idea what it would mean to me. My life would be complete."

As she looked into his dark eyes; the eyes of the only man she'd ever loved, she knew in her heart there was only one answer she could give.

"Yes," the words were uttered without any more thought, and it wasn't until his eyes lit up and a large smile emerged on his lips that she knew that she'd given him an answer. Her tears began to flow again, partly from the happiness of being with him again, of getting the thing she'd dreamed of over the years; a husband, a home, a baby. It was like a dream, but so bittersweet. She shook her head, as the tears continued to roll down her cheeks.

Damon stretched up and grabbed a couple tissues from the box on the end table. He gently wiped at her tears. "Hey, why are you crying?"

She sniffed and took the tissues from him. "Because, I'm happy and sad and... Oh God... It's so much. To lose you in a year, after finding you again..."

He pressed a finger to her lips. "It's not over yet honey. It's not. I'm going to fight this. I promise you. In the meantime, let's just enjoy our time together, whether it be a month, a year, or a lifetime. I promise work will never come before you again. Never."

Katrina threw herself at him, wrapped her arms around his neck and pushing him onto his back, with her straddling him. "Yes Damon. Yes, yes, yes!" She exclaimed running a trail of kisses up the side of his neck and then across his square jaw.

Laughing softly, Damon slid a hand to the back of her head, urging her lips to his, kissing her passionately. She gave in to him, moaning and running her hands over his shoulders. Her lips parted, inviting his tongue in as his cock began to rapidly expand between her legs and press against her stomach.

As their tongues danced, her entire body lit up with her desire for him. Her waiting and wanting him in combination to the mixture of intense emotions rushing through her was becoming overwhelming and she needed release from it all, and she knew the release came with the feel of his inside of her.

She pulled her lips from his, panting hard and pressed her forehead to his. They looked into each other's eyes, their breathing synchronizing. "If you make me wait another moment to make love to me I might just go insane Damon," she threatened, only partly joking.

In one, fast and fluid motion he flipped her over to her back and settled himself between her legs. She sighed. The feel of his body covering hers was divine and unlike earlier where the hard, cold tile pained her back, the soft fur of the rug was as comfortable as any bed.

Damon kissed her briefly and pulled up, a hand at either side of her head. The light from the fireplace danced off of the side of his face. She couldn't think of a more intimate and incredible atmosphere to make love to him for the first time - again.

"I love you, Katrina Alexander," he whispered, the conviction in his eyes even more convincing than his words.

Reaching up, Katrina touched the side of his face and smiled. "I never stopped loving you, Damon Garratt." She pulled his mouth back down to hers and closed her eyes as their lips touched. She breathed in deeply, basking in his feel, smell, and as their tongues united, his taste - champagne and spearmint.

He lowered himself onto her, as he reached between their bodies. His hand cupped her mound and she moaned against his mouth, while bucking against his hand. He slipped a finger between her wet folds and stroked her swollen nub. She cried out against his lips, her body moving under him. Her pussy clenched with need and her grip on his shoulders tightened, her fingernails digging into the hard muscle.

His finger moved from her clit and thrust into her core. She bucked a little harder, her body beginning to become a coil of tension. He added a second finger and began to stroke her clit with his thumb as his fingers fucked her. Her juices greeted his probing fingers and began to run down her ass. While his fingers stroked her inner wall in just the right place to make her body sing, his thumb continued its delicious torture of her clit.

Damon's lips left hers and began to work their way down the side of her neck, nipping lightly and flicking the sensitive flesh with his tongue. She was coming close, so close. She whimpered and moaned as she came closer and closer, her body becoming more and more tense. She was going to come, moments away. Sensing her impending orgasm, Damon lifted his head to look into her eyes.

"Come for me Kat. Come for me and you can have my cock," he murmured in her ear before pulling back to look into her eyes.

As she looked into his eyes, she came to the point of no return. The coil within her broke and she cried out as a wave of pleasure rushed over her and she was swept away in a tidal wave of satisfaction and relief.

Just when she thought the pleasure was over, he began to slowly push into her. Her back arched and she wrapped her legs around his waist as he sank deeper and deeper within her. She attempted to force him in faster, deeper, but he was in control and he was intent on savouring the feel of her wet, trembling pussy embracing his rock hard shaft.

"Damon. Oh God, Damon. Please, more." She gyrated under him, bucking against him, attempting to feel more of him as his cock spread her wider, filling her so deliciously full that it brought tears to her eyes. She clung tighter to him, pulling him down to her and burying her face against his neck.

"Damn Kat. My God, you have no idea how good you feel," he groaned, pushing himself in deeper, until three-quarters of his massive rod was penetrating her.

"Mmmm. I have a pretty good idea," she murmured, nipping at his shoulder and then working her way up his neck. He thrust hard and buried himself fully into her, balls deep. She cried out, her whole body tightening around him. Her breasts crushed against his massive chest as she pulled him deeper and holding tighter, needing to be as close to him as possible, not even wanting a fraction of an inch separating their bodies.

He remained embedded within her for a long moment, stretching her to her limits and relishing the feel of their bodies united. Just having him within her was driving her near insanity, even more than his excruciatingly slow initial thrust.

"If you don't start moving in me, I'm going to go mad," she groaned. Her body was humming, it was on the verge, but his non-movement had her suspended in a feeling of near pleasure and need, like she was at the finish line, but an invisible hand was holding her back, letting her see the finish, but not letting her indulge in the satisfaction of passing the line and breaking the ribbon.

Damon chuckled in return. "We can't have that." He slowly pulled out of her and shocked her by slamming into her hard and fast. The hard thrust, accompanied with his balls slapping against her pussy drove her over the edge she screamed out as she was sent spiralling over the edge of her desire once more.

"Damon! Damon! Oh-my-God, Damon!" She clawed at his back as he began to pound into her over and over, relentlessly taking pleasure in her needy pussy.

"Fuck. So good," he groaned nipping at the side of her neck, while never breaking pace. She moved, and arched under him, meeting each of his thrusts with her own, their bodies working in perfect harmony, giving and taking the pleasure they both so desperately needed.

She began to ascend the summit, yet again. Just when she thought she was going to hit the brink Damon stopped thrusting, his cock embedded deeply within her, and in one fast, fluid motion he flipped over to his back taking her with him. She yelped and giggled as she looked down at his smiling face and hungry eyes.

"Your turn. Take me over the edge sweetie," he instructed.

Sitting up on him, she placed her hands on his stomach, taking care to not put too much pressure near his incision. She began to move on him, and her smile widened as he closed his eyes and groaned low and deep in his throat. She could feel his cock thickening within her and knew he was getting close to coming for her. She began to move faster on him, moving her hips in a circular motion as she moved on him. As his moans rose in loudness and frequency, she found herself moving faster, harder, wanting to feel him unload his seed deep within her.

Did she? Was she going to have him cum in her?

She moved harder on him, taking the pleasure she needed as the head of his dick stroked her inner wall. Yes, she wanted him.

Wanted it. She needed to feel his seed filling her in an attempt to make their baby.

Placing her hands on his thighs behind her, she arched her back and let her head fall backwards, her blonde hair cascading down her back. She began to move on him at a frenzied pace, her body vibrating with her need. She needed to come again, almost as much as she needed him filling her.

"Oh yeah sweetie. Fuck me. Fuck me hard!" he groaned as his hands reached up and palmed her breasts. Her breasts fit perfectly in his hands and her nipples hardened as his fingers worked them, pinching and rolling them into peaks.

"God yes! Fill me Damon. Fill me please."

She could feel his eyes on her, watching her breasts bounce each time she slammed down onto him, but couldn't open her eyes to look down to verify. She was coming to her breaking point as she felt him preparing to release. His balls tightened under her, he was moments away.

"If you don't want too."

She opened her eyes and fell forward. "I want it," she groaned closing her eyes and claiming his lips. As their lips touched he thrust up into her and groaned against her mouth as a fury of his cum was unleashed within her. Feeling the beat of his stream of cum slamming against her inner walls sent her over the edge and she echoed his moan against his mouth as her pussy clenched and then released, milking his cock for every ounce of his seed while unleashing a flood of her juices to greet his shaft.

She had no idea how long she was suspended in that glorious moment of pleasure, seconds, minutes. She had no idea how long it had been, but when she pulled her mouth away from his, gasping hard and collapsing on top of him, she was exhausted, spent and completely sated.

She trembled over him as she relaxed, in no rush to remove his rapidly depleting cock from her core. He felt good within her. It was where he belonged.

Chapter 11

Katrina sighed softly, as she slowly woke to the feel of her hair being stroked. A soft smile touched her lips and she debated with herself on whether she was going to wake up or not. The empty feeling in her stomach and the insane urge to pee became the deciding factor. She needed to get up, regardless of how good it felt to have Damon stroking her hair while she slept.

"Mmmmm. Didn't you get enough last night?" They'd had four rounds of love making the previous evening, taking them well into the morning. They had finally fallen to sleep under the blanket he'd draped over her shoulders earlier that evening with the fire frolicking in the background.

He didn't answer, but continued to stroke her hair, but getting a little more rough, yanking at a lock of hair with force. "Ouch! Damon!" She slowly opened her eyes, pulling her hair from his grip and let out an earth-shattering scream as her eyes didn't focus on Damon's, but two chocolate brown eyes of a small monkey.

The monkey leapt back and onto the back of the sofa, replicating her scream and placing its hands over its mouth.

She screamed a second time, still in shock as she scrambled to her feet clutching the blanket around her. The monkey also screamed a second time, a blood curdling high-pitched scream and began to bounce around the room, its eyes wild in terror, highlighted by its white furry face.

Struggling to lower her heart rate she took several deep breaths in and slowly released them as she watched the monkey, who was also beginning to settle down. Perched on the back of the rocking chair, its toes curled around the rails and it began to eye her with suspicion and hostility.

Once she got over her initial surprise at being woken up by a monkey stroking her hair, Katrina had to admit the little guy was pretty cute. It reminded her of that monkey they had on the television show *Friends*. For the life of her she couldn't remember the monkey's name, but it was definitively the same species. A giggle escaped her lips when she noticed he was wearing a diaper.

Deciding she wasn't a threat, the monkey jumped down from the rocking chair located across the room and made his way over to her. He jumped up onto the leather sofa and perched himself on the back so he was almost eye to eye with her.

"Kimmy!"

Still slightly riled up from her surprise wake-up, the appearance of a petite blonde woman bursting into the den had Katrina jumping in surprise and screaming for a third time. The monkey, who she now knew to be named, 'Kimmy' also screamed, while jumping up and down on the sofa.

"There you are." The woman rushed over to the monkey, virtually ignoring Katrina, and gathered the animal into her arms.

The monkey climbed up onto the woman's shoulder and perched herself, its dark eyes still locked onto Katrina.

The blonde woman turned to look at Katrina, whose face burned with her embarrassment. Where was Damon? Why did he leave her there sleeping on the floor to be fondled by monkeys and stared at by...

She quickly surveyed the other woman, who was dressed in a light brown uniform, with a nametag identifying her as Faith, and that she worked at the Houston South Zoo. She let out a loud sigh. So this was the zookeeper. She didn't *look* like much of a zookeeper; she looked like she belonged on a cover of a magazine. It was apparent she wasn't wearing a stitch of make-up and she was still a stunning woman. Katrina felt a pang of jealousy. This woman was here every day?

Faith stared back at her. She didn't seem to be any more pleased to see Katrina as Katrina was to see her. The zookeeper had a thing for him; there was no doubt in Katrina's mind. Had he had a fling with her too? He'd admitted to having a fling with his secretary, did he fuck all his female staff?

*****

"What's going on?" Damon rushed into the room and skidded to a halt as he watched the two women eye each other, sizing each other up. *Ahhhh shit*, he groaned inwardly. He'd been busy in his office and hadn't expected for Faith to enter the house. Usually when she came in she announced herself, she hadn't today.

Both women turned their attention to him and Faith was the first to speak. "Damon. Hi, I ummm... Kimmy decided to explore and I lost her." She shrugged. "Found her in here with..." She turned her eyes back to Katrina.

Letting out a loud sigh, Damon nodded as he walked over to Katrina, slipped an arm around her waist and pulled her tight. "Well, Faith this is my fiancée, Katrina."

Faith's smile fell and her expression went blank. He knew she was taking the news hard. She had a thing for him for close to a year now, he hadn't encouraged her, but at the same time he hadn't discouraged her either. He enjoyed the younger woman's company, but at the same time he didn't have that 'click' feeling towards her so never pursued anything more than friendship with her.

Katrina cuddled up against him, a smile forming on her lips as she glanced up at him and caught his gaze.

"Oh," the zookeeper finally managed to get out once she got over her shock of the engagement. "That was fast. I didn't even think you were dating someone?" She frowned, keeping her eyes focused on him.

"Yeah, well..." He cleared his throat.

"Nice to meet you, Faith. I look forward to getting to know you better." Holding the blanket she had wrapped around her tight to her chest, Katrina extended her hand to Faith. The younger woman accepted her hand, giving it a quick shake.

"Good to meet you, Katrina." She motioned towards the door. "I'm going to leave now. The animals are taken care of for the day." She scampered away with Kimmy seated on her shoulder before Damon could respond, closing the door firmly behind her.

Katrina slipped from his embrace and he didn't have to look down at her face to know she was angry. As he lowered his gaze to hers, sure enough, there was fire in her blue eyes and not the kind that was in them last night when they were making love. She was indeed pissed.

"Did you fuck that one too?"

Damon fought to keep a smile from emerging on his lips. He'd forgotten how sexy she was when she was angry and how much of a temper she had when other women were involved.

"Well." She tapped her bare foot as she waited for his response.

"My God, you're sexy when you're jealous," he couldn't help but tease.

"I. Am. Not. Jealous," she hissed, poking him in the chest to accent each word.

A bout of laughter overtook him. He couldn't help it. She was just too damned cute and it brought back so many memories.

"This isn't funny. I'm serious," she protested, but a grin was fighting to emerge on her lips, he could see the corners of her lips lifting. "You left me alone to be fondled by monkeys."

"We've been engaged for less than twelve hours and already we're fighting." He tisked at her softly, and pulled her into his arms.

"We're not fighting," she defended, the smile breaking out on her lips. "I was asking a question."

He laughed again and lowered his lips to hers. "Uh-huh. I'd forgotten how jealous you get."

"I'm not jealous, but she gave me a look and you admitted to having that fling with your secretary." She kissed him back, releasing the blanket and sliding her hands up his chest and lacing her fingers behind his neck, pressing her naked body against him.

His cock immediately sprang to life, pressing against his jeans. He wanted to take her again. He'd been having a hard time trying to get any work what-so-ever done that morning because his mind kept going back to her and their night together.

He gave himself a moment to run his hands down her back and caress her bottom, while he deepened the kiss, his tongue searching out hers. He was tempted to pick her up, toss her onto the sofa, strip naked and spend the afternoon filling her over and over, but he had stuff to do and it wouldn't get done indulging his cock, no matter how much he wanted to.

With great reluctance he pulled away from her, and stepped back. "Honey, I gotta run into Houston for a few hours so you'll have to entertain yourself. Explore the house. Make yourself at home. If you want to go into the city, maybe do some shopping I can give you one of my credit cards and you may shop to your heart's content. Just take whatever car you want, the keys to them all are in the top left hand drawer of my desk."

Her face fell, disappointment registering in her expression.

"It's not a business thing, I promise. You'll like it. I just gotta do this on my own. But I won't be long."

Her smile reappeared, but not as bright. She fingered the collar of his light blue, pinstripe, button down shirt. "Okay. I'll stay here. But you're all mine tonight?"

He hooked his index finger under her chin, tilted her face upwards and he kissed her softly. "All yours. In fact, there is going to be a delivery in a few hours for you and I have something really special planned for us."

"Really?"

"Really," he confirmed.

*****

"Just make sure it happens, Kevin." Damon ended the call, not waiting for Kevin's reply as he pulled his Lamborghini into a parking slot in front of Gamble and Fennel fine jewellers. They had the best of the best in Houston when it came to engagement rings. He'd rather of had one custom made for her, but considering they were on a time crunch he had to make due.

Getting out of the car, he closed the door, locked it with a press of a button and made his way into the lavish boutique. He immediately walked past the display cases towards the back of the shop. He'd already called ahead and apparently they were supposed to have the perfect ring for him.

As he made his way towards the back of the store his eyes caught sight of a stunning yellow sapphire pendant suspended from a diamond chain set in platinum, with matching diamond pear drop diamond earrings. They were perfect for her and would match the yellow satin gown he was having delivered to the house this morning. Without even bothering to look at the price he kept moving towards the back counter where he was supposed to meet with a man named Ralph Gamble, the owner of the shop.

As he approached, an elderly gentleman entered the showroom from the back to greet him.

"Mr. Gamble," Damon asked, extending his hand to the gentleman.

"Yes, Sir. And you would be Damon?"

"I would. Before you bring me the ring," he turned and pointed to the case in the center of the room featuring the yellow sapphire necklace, "Could you have someone wrap the necklace in the center showcase for me along with the earrings and a matching bracelet."

"Of course, Sir." The jeweller motioned to one of the younger female saleswomen who was within hearing range. "Please box the Esmeralda diamond set, Jenny." Reaching under the counter he produced two velvet cases. The first he opened displayed a perfectly cut 5ct oval diamond in a platinum setting. The second featured a matching platinum wedding band set with three diamonds on the top of each of the bands. The sparkling of the diamonds was mesmerizing under the soft florescent lighting.

"Your fiancée is a very lucky woman," Ralph commented, motioning to the rings. "These are some of the best cut diamonds you can find anywhere."

Damon smiled as he removed the ring from the case and inspected it a little closer. The light danced off of the edges of the diamond. The funny thing was that Katrina would have been happy with a ring from the showcase of Wal-Mart. She'd never been the kind of woman to demand much. She'd been struggling for so many years financially, now that she was in his life, as far as he was concerned she would only get the very best from now on. She deserved that much at the very least, because what she was offering to give him was priceless.

Chapter 12

"Delivery for Miss Alexander," a young FedEx delivery man announced as Katrina opened the front door. Juggling a long white box under his arm, the delivery man thrust an electronic signing device at her, pointing to the spot for her signature. "Sign here."

Katrina signed and accepted the white box secured together with a large silver ribbon and bow. She closed the door with her hip, as she pulled the card from under the ribbon. She made her way into the living room and placed the box onto the oval coffee table. She then opened the envelope and pulled out the card.

For tonight, I know you'll look amazing in it. Love you, Damon.

A wide grin spread across her lips as she opened the box to reveal a yellow satin gown. Standing, she gently pulled it out of the box, and examined it at arm's length. The dress was floor length and sleeveless, with a v-cut that dipped low, appeared to be form-fitting and flared out at the bottom. The satin was so soft in her hands that she couldn't resist the urge to bring it to her cheek and rub her face against it. It was beautiful, easily the most stunning dress she'd ever owned. Along with it, the box contained a matching purse and golden, glittering strappy heels.

"You got the dress I see."

Spinning around, her grin widened as she set her eyes on Damon, looking as sexy as ever in a black suit, with the blue pinstriped shirt he'd been wearing earlier. "Thank you so much. I love it!" she squealed rushing across the room and into his arms. "You don't need to buy me stuff. I'm happy just to be with you again." She pressed herself against him and kissed his lips lightly. "Thank you, thank you, thank you."

Damon chuckled, "You're welcome."

She stepped back and examined the dress again, feeling like a princess and praying it would fit. "I really don't need you buying me stuff."

Damon's smile faded and he shrugged. "In that case, I guess I can take this back."

Turning back to him, her eyes quickly caught sight of a brown bag dangling from a string on his finger. "Well, we can make one more exception." She rushed back to the coffee table and gently placed the dress back into the box, feeling like a child on Christmas day.

She spun back around to see Damon standing behind her, the parcel for her still suspended from his index finger. Taking the bag, her heart rate accelerated as she peeped inside.

"Well, open it!" Her eyes met his and she could see his excitement was at par with hers. As kids he'd always loved buying her little things. Neither one of them had much in the way of money so they couldn't afford much, but it hadn't been about the money. It had always been about the thought.

Sitting back down and with trembling fingers she pulled out a medium sized narrow box. Opening the white box she was confronted with a black velvet jewellery case.

"Damon, you really don't need to spoil me," she said as she slowly opened the box. Despite her protest, she loved that he had.

"In that case, I can take it..."

She slapped his hands away from the box. "No. You already bought it."

Chuckling, Damon sat back onto the sofa and watched intently as she continued opening the box and gasped. Katrina's blue eyes widened, hardly being able to believe what she was looking at. The diamonds sparkled unlike anything she'd ever seen before. She didn't even have to know the price to know the contents of the box cost more than she'd make with two years wage, at the hotel.

Her legs felt weak under her and she sat down next to Damon, as she fingered the stunning necklace. The diamond bangle bracelet and earrings were equally as stunning, but it was the large yellow sapphire that kept her eyes drawn to it.

"This is too much Damon," she gasped as she continued to finger the beautiful diamonds. "I don't know what to say."

Damon took the box from her and set it onto the coffee table, next to the dress. Grabbing her hips, he pulled her over to him. Katrina stretched out over him and kissed him softly. "Thank you."

"You're welcome." He ran his fingers through her long locks, taking a moment to watch the golden strands falling from his fingertips. "There is one thing you can do for me."

Katrina nodded enthusiastically. "Yes, anything."

"Put the dress and jewellery on. We have a little function to go to. I tried to get out of it, but it's a charity thing and it was strongly suggested we attend." His hands snaked their way around her waist, holding her secure to him.

Katrina's spirits fell. She hated the idea of sharing him this evening. She was being greedy, she knew she was, but after the previous evening with him the only thing she could think about was the feel of his hard, naked body against hers. She'd been itching to masturbate all day, but she'd restrained herself waiting for him.

His grin widened upon seeing her disappointment. "It'll be a couple hours at the most; we'll try to escape within an hour."

She nodded. "Okay." She ran her index finger down the front of his shirt. "And then you're all mine for the rest of the evening?"

"To do whatever you want with," he confirmed, brushing his lips across her temple.

She wiggled onto him, and relished the sound of his sharp intake of breath and the feel of his growing dick against her. "Mmmmm. You're making it too tempting an offer to refuse."

"Good." He gave her ass a quick, but smarting slap, making her yelp in both surprise and because of the sharp burn that came from the slap.

Pulling back and getting to her feet she growled at him, eyes narrowing. "You'll pay for that mister."

Damon laughed, mischief dancing in his dark eyes. "Oh promises, promises." Getting to his feet, Damon picked up the box with the dress in it and nodded towards the jewellery case. "Come on. Let's get ready for the ball, baby."

She cocked a brow up at him. "A ball. Are you serious?" She grabbed her beautiful new necklace, earrings and bracelet.

"As a heart attack, sweet thang," he attempted a Southern drawl, but failed miserably. He attempted to give her rump another smack, but she scampered out of the way and turned the tables on him, giving him a taste of his own medicine, smacking him soundly on the rear.

He made a soft 'omph' sound and growled at her. "Oh, you're going to pay for that missy."

"Gotta catch me first!" Without waiting for a response she clutched her jewels to her chest and sprinted from the room on her way towards the stairwell leading to the bedrooms on the second floor. She heard laughter behind her, along with his heavy footsteps in hot pursuit. She doubted she'd mind all that much if he caught her, but at least wanted to make him work for it - if even just a little bit.

*****

Katrina stepped into the satin gown and wiggled as she pulled it up and slipped the straps over her shoulders. How he knew what her size was still baffled her, she'd gained some poundage since they were younger, but it seemed everything Damon did was perfect... Well, except for the idea of driving the Ferrari to the lookout, but she'd cut him some slack on that considering he was trying to be romantic.

Brushing her loose hair over one shoulder, she reached behind her and attempted to pull the zipper up, but was only able to get it part of the way. She groaned her frustration and sighed. Leaving her massive dressing room, which was easily as big as her apartment in Bangor, she entered the bedroom she was going to be sharing with Damon to search him out.

She stopped in mid-stride when she laid eyes on him. Standing in the middle of the bedroom, adjusting a cuff-link was Damon wearing a tuxedo and looking so drop dead sexy that it took her breath away, rendering her speechless.

He turned his eyes toward her and a wide smile broke out on his face.

"I... Ummmm." Katrina frowned. Her words seemed to leave her.

Damon cocked a brow at her, his grin widening.

"Yeah, I..." She spun around. "Zipper." Holding her hair up, she waited, breath held. She was about to turn back around when she heard his footsteps behind her.

Damon touched her shoulders, sending a shiver through her, igniting the fire between her legs. Leaning into her, he bent down and grazed his lips up the side of her neck. "You smell incredible," he murmured, his lips moving closer to her ear lobe.

She closed her eyes and leaned back against the hard wall of his chest. His cologne overtook her, sweeping her up. She longed to lose herself in his arms and in the smell of his cologne. Damn, she wished they didn't have whatever charity function it was that they were going to attend and that they could just spend the evening naked and in each others' arms.

"So do you," she managed to choke out.

He straightened back up and slowly tugged her zipper up, the bodice of her dress tightening around her modest breasts. "Stay there a second and I'll put the necklace on you."

Chewing at her lower lip, she nodded. Excitement welled up within her. She really was going to be the princess of the ball. Her... Katrina Alexander... a banquet server for a hotel in Bangor was being lavished in diamonds and beautiful clothing. It had to be a dream. Any minute she'd wake up and it would be all a cruel dream and she would be going back to her life as a server, avoiding the landlord because she didn't have the rent for him.

Damon stepped up behind her and then slipped the diamond necklace around her neck, the yellow sapphire landed just over her breastbone. Despite her building excitement over going to whatever event he was taking her to, she was craving his touch, the apex between her legs becoming increasingly wet.

"Okay," he whispered, his lips less than an inch from her ear. "Turn around. I have another surprise for you."

Another surprise? She doubted she could handle many more. She turned slowly, allowing her hair to slip from her fingers and cascade down her back. She was once again struck speechless as Damon fell to one knee with a small velvet box in his hand.

He cleared his throat and began to look slightly nervous. A smile tugged at the corners of her lips at seeing him looking so uncomfortable.

"Last night I really didn't get to do this properly." He motioned towards the bedroom. "This isn't exactly the way I'd envisioned proposing to you either, but," he sighed, "It is what it is."

"This is perfect Damon." And she meant it.

His body relaxed slightly as he took her left hand in his. "Katrina, when I think back over my life. And I've been doing that a lot lately, the only time I really felt happiness was when I was with you. You were my best friend, my first love..." He chuckled, glancing up and catching her eyes, "My *only* love. I swear to you now that you'll never want or need for anything again. You, and if we're lucky our baby, will be my world. I want to give you the world Katrina. I've loved you from the day we met and I'll love you for the rest of our lives and beyond."

Oh God. The tears. She fought them back, knowing the make-up she'd spent a half an hour to apply would be for nothing if she let the flood gates open.

"So." He opened the case and she gasped. She'd never seen a diamond so perfect. He pulled the ring from the case and stuffed it into his outer jacket pocket. "So will you, Katrina Alexander, do me the immense honour of being my wife?"

"Of course. I love you Damon. Of course!" He slipped the ring onto her finger and stood.

Oh, here we go!

"Damon Garratt, you bastard." The tears began to stream down her face trailing long streaks of black in their wake. She sniffed and grabbed for a tissue, trying to salvage her make-up. "You've made me ruin my make-up!"

He chuckled, pulling her into his arms. "I'm sorry baby."

"You are not!"

He laughed louder.

Sliding her hands up his chest she laced her fingers behind his neck and pressed her body tight against his. "Are you sure there's no way we can skip the thingie and just stay here?" She kissed the side of his neck lightly, and he groaned.

"Wish we could. Besides, you look stunning. We don't want that to go to waste."

She kissed his neck a second time, hoping to entice him.

"Not going to work woman." Despite his words, his cock told a different story as it began to harden against his stomach. He groaned a second time as her hand slipped between them to stroke the ridge of his shaft over the layers of clothing. "No. No, no, no." Damon pulled away and stepped out of her embrace. He tapped the bridge of her nose. "Later. Besides, we won't stay long. We have a long day tomorrow, and the following day..." His voice trailed off leaving her anxious to hear what he had in mind.

"Which is..."

He shrugged. "I'm not at liberty to say, Miss Alexander."

"Damon!" She heard the high pitched whiney note her tone took and winced, but he didn't seem to be bothered.

His grin widened and he shook his head, determination in his gaze. "Nothing you can do will change my mind, so you might as well finish getting ready. Don't want to be late."

Katrina sighed and turned towards the large mirror connected to the double dresser. *Oh-my-God, I look a mess.* Her smeared make-up made her look like a crazed clown.

"Ten minutes sweetie. Then we gotta leave."

Ten minutes to fix this! She groaned and prayed she could get cleaned up fast enough.

Chapter 13

Damon could feel the nervousness and tension within Katrina as she clung to his arm and they entered the ballroom.

"I'm freaking scared Damon," she whispered as they began to descend the black marble staircase that lead to a ballroom with roughly three hundred people fraternizing. There were twenty-five tables set up with twelve place settings per table. Dinner was to be served in a half hour with an up-and-coming blues band providing the music for the evening, after the supper.

"Why?" He glanced down at her frowning.

"Look at all the women. They're gorgeous. And they all look so..." She nibbled at her lower lip, considering her next words.

"Snotty?" he offered.

She laughed, her body relaxing somewhat next to his. "Yeah. But they're all nice people right?"

Damon's eyes surveyed the crowd with seriousness and then shook his head. "Most of them are pompous assholes, but they're business associates and people that can be useful so we have to endure I'm afraid." She looked up at him and caught his gaze. "And play nice."

She rolled her eyes at him. "I work as a server; I spend a good chunk of time pretending to like people I can't stand each week. Nothing new here. But it feels like they're watching us."

"Besides, they're not watching us. They're watching you," he leaned down and whispered.

"Oh and that's supposed to make me feel better?"

He shook his head. "Nope."

"Why watching me?"

"Cause I never bring a date to these things and you're easily the most stunning woman in this place."

"Why not?"

He frowned. "Why not what?"

"Why do you never bring dates to these things?"

"Because I rarely date. Never had time." He lowered his voice substantially and leaned into her. "Oh, and they don't know about the cancer so lets keep it that way."

Her smile fell, and he hated his words were the reason and that he had to remind her of his condition, but if some of the people in the room knew of his medical problems then it could cause him some issues with a number of the big deals he had in the works. Their continued ignorance on the issue was imperative.

"Okay."

"But, the engagement is completely open for discussion, and as soon as they see the ring, I assure you they won't be reserved enough to not ask."

"Damon Garratt, did you give me the ring just so I could show it off?" she teased.

He laughed. "I gave you the ring so they would stop suspecting I'm gay."

Katrina joined in his laughter as they reached the ballroom floor. "You're joking. Why would they ever think that?"

He wished he was. There had been one event where he'd been propositioned by a male business associate. It had been awkward to say the least and he was just grateful the other man had been drinking rather heavily. They brushed it off as something the other man said out of drunkin' stupidity. "Hmmm. Well, I never show up with a date to any of these things. No one has any knowledge of any girlfriends in my history. It's not that hard of a conclusion to jump to."

Her grasp onto his arm tightened and she snuggled tighter to him as the first couple approached them - his first in commend Kevin Gilbert and his wife Judith.

"Damon, how are you?" Kevin extended his hand to Damon, but his eyes were on Katrina. "So this is your friend from Bangor?"

Damon nodded. "Kevin and Judith, this is Katrina Alexander, soon to be Katrina Garratt."

Kevin's smile faded into a tight grimace. "What do you mean?"

Damon would have laughed at Kevin's reaction if it hadn't been so insulting, but he was sure this was only the first of similar reactions. "I mean, I proposed last night and she said yes. So we're getting married."

Kevin's eyes shot over to Katrina. "Congratulations. That's great news." His wife mimicked his sentiment, but with a little more truthfulness in her congratulations.

"I think so."

"Katrina, do you mind if I steal Damon away for a moment?"

Katrina shot Damon a terrified look. Giving her hand, resting on his arm a reassuring squeeze, he nodded.

She gave Kevin a smile and nodded. "Of course." She reluctantly released his arm.

"Don't worry Damon, I'll keep her busy while you two talk shop." Judith, a tall, slender woman of her mid-twenties stated slipping an arm around Katrina's shoulders.

Katrina and Damon locked gazes for a moment and the fear in her eyes lessened slightly when he mouthed, *I love you.* Turning his attention back to Kevin, the two men walked out of earshot. Damon didn't have long to ponder what Kevin's concern was, he lunged right into it.

"When did this happen?"

"Last night."

"Rather fast, don't you think?"

Damon chuckled. "Considering I should have done it a decade ago, I wouldn't say so."

"It's going to be a long engagement?"

"For sure. We can't get our marriage licence until tomorrow, so we wouldn't be married until Tuesday. So there's going to be a couple days before the wedding."

In the process of taking a sip of his drink, Kevin began to choke. His eyes - which had begun to water from his choking fit - jerking up to meet Damon's in disbelief. "You can't be serious! You're getting a pre-nup I assume."

A part of Damon felt he should be angry at Kevin's intrusive questions, but he cut him a little slack. It was a shock and under other circumstances he imagined he'd be as shocked as Kevin was. Perhaps even asking similar questions.

"No pre-nup."

Damon was about to speak, then thought twice about it. Damon could see him considering his next question. "Do you think it's wise not to? What if she's taking advantage of your," he cleared his throat averting his gaze and glancing over at the two women chatting, "of your... situation."

Damon took a deep breath in and slowly released it, giving himself a moment to gather his thoughts before saying something he shouldn't out of anger. Grasping the other man's shoulder he leaned into him and their eyes locked. "I'm going to make this very clear to you. Katrina is not taking advantage of my *condition*. I'm marrying her because I love her and I have no desire to explain our relationship any further than that, so I expect her to be treated with the respect that you would treat me in. She's going to be around a lot and learning about the company, catching up to speed on every aspect. I expect you'll assist with her with whatever she needs."

"You're serious?" A look of distress crossed his features and gleamed in his blue eyes.

"Have you ever known me to joke when it comes to my company?"

*****

"So, what do you think, so far?"

Katrina sighed as she slipped into Damon's arms and held tight to him as the blues band played a soft, sexy melody. "I'm actually exhausted. All these people... They seem so..."

"Phoney?" he offered, his lips close to her ear and his voice so low that only she could hear. The warmth of his breath tickled her neck and sent a tremor of need through her.

She nodded. "Very. Though I will admit that I kinda enjoyed the look of envy in the women's eyes when they found out we're engaged." That was an understatement. She'd loved it - relished it.

When they were growing up, her family had lived paycheck to paycheck. She never did without, but she never had the brand names or the finer things many of the girls had. She'd spent a lot of time envious of the other girls, things they had and vacations they got to take with their families. Tonight she got to be the woman who had everything, but most importantly, who had the most amazing man on her arm. She felt like the prom queen. And it was all because of him.

He pulled back and smiled. "So you're happy?"

Happy couldn't begin to describe what she was feeling, despite the dark cloud that was looming over their relationship. "Very happy." She pressed herself a little tighter to him and unable to resist herself and unconcerned about the people around her, she brushed her lips across his.

"Mmmmm. Well, the dinner is over and I think we've made a long enough appearance that if we wanted to take off I'm sure no one would notice."

Katrina looked around them; several sets of eyes were watching their every move - Kevin and Judith in particular. "Oh, I think they'd notice."

"Let me rephrase this. I want to leave and don't care if they notice. But we can stay if you're having a good time and would like. Keep in mind you'll be attending thousands of these things with me in the coming years."

She wrapped her arms around his neck and nuzzled against his neck. Years of this. Of him. She couldn't think of anything she'd want more. "Then let's get out of here."

His body relaxed, he released her and slowly put some distance between them. "Fantastic. I was hoping you'd say that. This past hour all I could think about was taking you home and getting you out of that dress." Grabbing her hand he led her to the exit as he pulled his valet ticket from the inner pocket of his jacket.

He passed the ticket to the young man at the door, who thanked him and disappeared into the parking garage.

"Shouldn't we have least said good-bye to Kevin."

Damon huffed and gave his head a curt shake.

Katrina had noticed his demeanour with Kevin had gotten rather cool after they'd taken off to have a brief discussion. It made her wonder what was said between them, though she didn't want to ask. If he wanted her to know, he'd tell her. Maybe it was business, but she suspected it had to do with her and their quickie engagement and wedding plans.

Which brought her to the question of what he had planned for the wedding? A small ceremony on the edge of a cliff overlooking an ocean at some country club. A simple ceremony in front of a judge in Houston? She was anxious to find out and he seemed to be rather closed-mouthed about his plans.

"So where are we getting married anyhow?" It was a long shot in the dark, but what the hell; she'd give it a try.

He glanced down at her and a smirk touched his lips. "Oh, that's for me to know and you to find out."

Before she had a chance to inquire further the valet pulled up with the top down on Damon's canary yellow Lamborghini Aventador.

"I think this is my favourite car of yours Damon."

"Car of *ours*," he corrected as they reached the car and he passed the valet a tip. Katrina had no idea how much he gave the young man, but whatever it was the valet seemed thrilled to get it. He opened the passenger door for her and she slid in. Closing the door once she was seated, she watched him as he walked around the front of the car to slip in behind the wheel. Like a hundred times before now, she was amazed at how amazingly sexy he'd become. She'd seen the women at the event watch him with lust in their eyes. All he would have had to do was say the word and she was sure the vast majority of them would have happily left their dates and bent over any table just for a fast, hard fucking from him.

And he was hers. All hers.

Within ten minutes they were travelling down the highway, with the warm night air blowing her hair wildly around her head and into her face. Her eyes lowered to his hand on the shifter and then to his lap and more importantly what was contained within his black trousers.

Her hand slid onto his leg, half-way between his knee and his groin. His body tensed under her hand and he glanced over at her, eyebrow raised. "If you're trying to seduce me into telling you where we're getting married then it'll take a little more convincing than that."

"Is that a challenge Mr. Garratt?"

He shrugged, shifting his eyes back to the road. "I'm just saying... That information is vaulted."

Katrina's hand slid a little higher on his thigh. "Vaulted? Are you sure?"

Chapter 14

Damon's cock jerked alive in his pants as her hand crept higher and higher on his leg. "You know it's dangerous to be teasing a man who's driving."

She shot his a sassy look and cocked a brow up at him. "That so?"

"It's a safety issue," he teased.

She swiped her tongue over her lower lip, making it shine, calling to him, urging him to kiss her hard and deep. He took a deep breath in, trying to ignore the feelings sweeping over him. It was an impossible task. He surveyed their surroundings as her hand made it to his groin and cupped his balls, squeezing gently.

"Kat," he groaned, "Stop or I swear to God I'll stop this car and fuck you on the damned hood." It wasn't an idle threat he'd been fighting his erection all night, especially when they'd begun to dance and she had rubbed her body up against his. At the time he hadn't been sure if she'd been doing it on purpose or by mistake, but he was suspecting it had been on purpose. It would serve the little bugger right if he followed through with the threat.

Ah-hah! There's a spot coming up! She gave his balls another squeeze and he flicked on the blinker, more out of habit than for the benefit of other drivers. The highway they were on was somewhat out of the way and rarely used, but it was the quickest way back to his, correction, *their* ranch.

"What are you doing?" Katrina didn't move her hand, but her caressing his balls stopped as she sat up straighter in the passenger seat. Alarm began to register in her eyes and he grinned.

"Going to show you what happens when you tease," he explained as the car slowed into the parking lot of an abandoned gas station. The gas station was a little *Texas Chainsaw Massacre* in style, but it would do.

Katrina snatched her hand back and laced her fingers on her lap. "Seriously, what are we doing here? It's creepy."

"Adds to the excitement, don't you think? Besides, if I notice any large men wearing someone else's face skin as a mask I'll pull out and get us out of here."

Giggling, she gave him a slap on the shoulder. "Come on Damon. Let's get out of here. I promise I'll behave until we get home."

"Too late now, Kat." Damon slowed the car and parked it out of sight of the highway, the worn and neglected brick building blocking the view of them from anyone passing by on the highway.

"But what if someone comes? We almost got caught at the lookout."

"I'm pretty sure Mark isn't in Houston," he teased shutting off the car and undoing his seat belt.

Kat rolled her eyes at him, but a flicker of desire appeared in her blue eyes.

"Since I'm such a nice guy, I'll give you two choices. Either you can be a good little girl, get over here and fuck me or we get out, I hike up your dress and fuck you from behind over the hood."

She undid her safety belt and squirmed in her seat, a grin appearing on her lips. Her eyes went to his lap and then to the hood of the car and back again as if making up her mind.

Leaning forward, Damon undid his tuxedo jacket and shrugged out of it as he pushed the seat back as far as possible. "Come here." He reached across the shifter box and ran his finger alone her jawbone and then traced her lower lip with his thumb. She caught his thumb between her teeth and sucked it into her mouth. His cock jerked and he groaned, imagining the feel of her lips around his shaft.

She released his thumb with a sexy grin touching her lips, then reached across the gearbox and undid his pants. He moaned softly as she pulled down his pants and boxer briefs. Gripping his balls in one hand she leaned forward and lowered her lips to the head of his dick.

"Okay... This... This works too..." he moaned out as her tongue lashed out and flicked at the pre-cum seeping from the tip of his shaft.

Damon raked his fingers through her silken strands, brushing her hair away from her face so he could watch her lips and tongue as it taunted and teased his rod. She circled the head of his cock with her tongue and then gently pulled the head into her mouth sending a jolt of pleasure through him. His cock turned rock solid under her teasing tongue and his hand fisted her locks as he bit down the urge to thrust up into her mouth.

Grasping his balls she began to massage him, as her tongue ran down the underside of his dick and then slowly back up. She repeated the process and then took the head into her mouth, her tongue circling and taunting. Another shiver rushed through him and he groaned out loud. His groan urged her on as she took him in further, moaning softly. The humming sensation was like a symphony of pleasure running through him, bringing him closer and closer.

"You have no idea how good that feels," he groaned.

Releasing his cock, she glanced up, her eyes full of hunger that nearly sent him over the edge and caught his gaze. "I have an idea. But I'm sure you'll remind me later on."

He ran his fingers through her hair. "Is that a request?"

"It's a fact."

Not waiting for him to answer she took him in fully, the head of his cock slamming against her throat. Closing his eyes, he moaned loudly and began to thrust up into her mouth, allowing the pleasure to run freely through him as her head began to bob into his lap; her dainty hand gripped around the base of his shaft moving in sync with her mouth.

Each time her mouth reached the tip of his cock, she'd swirl her tongue along to top, before taking him back in - an extra tease that was driving him near insanity for her. His balls began to get heavy and harden to a point that was near pain. He was rushing close, too close.

"Oh fuck me. Oh Fuck Kat. Stop!" He was going to come and the last thing he wanted was to come without feeling her pussy around him. His eyes sprang open as he hit the summit and he jerked back in the seat.

Sensing his distress, Katrina sat up and wiped her chin which had a drop of his cum shimmering on it with the back of her hand. "Good?" she teased as she flopped back into her seat, hiked up her dress, hooked her thumbs into the waistband of her skimpy black lace panties and pulled them down her legs and tossed them onto the dash of the car.

Good didn't even begin to describe the feeling of her mouth on him.

"I don't want to waste a baby making opportunity," she explained.

Damon laughed. "I can't agree more."

Hiking the long skirt of her gown up until it was bunched at her waist and her mound wonderfully exposed, she struggled to get over the gearbox and to straddle his lap. It was both arousing and funny as hell. He wasn't sure if he wanted to laugh louder or blow his load before she could even take him in. He chose to laugh.

"Oh, so you're finding this amusing?" she asked, a grin touching her lips.

"Funny, exciting, sexy-as-hell. I'm finding this situation a number of things."

She settled onto him, his shaft peeping out between their bodies. She grasped his cock and began to stroke him.

His laughter immediately stopped and a low, feral groan escaped him. "More aroused now," he admitted, sliding a hand to the back of her neck and urging her mouth down to his. Her scent - sweet roses - drifted to his nose as she leaned into him and their lips met.

She sighed against his lips as the kiss deepened and her free hand fisted the front of his shirt. Adjusting herself onto him, she ran the head of his cock back and forth between her velvety folds. Her soft, wet folds felt like heaven, enticing his shaft, begging for him to sink deep within her soft core.

"I need you Damon," she moaned before kissing him harder, denying him a chance to respond as she thrust her tongue into his mouth, searching out his. As their tongues touched, sending a spike of desire through him he slid his hands up her bare outer thighs and pulled her down onto him. He couldn't have waited another moment to take her if he wanted to; his dick's demands were too strong.

She lined the head of his cock to her entrance and slowly eased him into her. Her pussy spread to accommodate his girth as she slowly took him into her. He attempted to pull her down onto him faster, harder, but she wasn't allowing it.

Pulling her lips from his she caught his gaze, his own desire reflected in her stunning blue eyes, as she slammed down onto him completely, her moist throbbing core surrounding every last inch of his manhood.

She whimpered and wiggled on him.

"Oh dear God," he groaned. "Give me a moment." The last thing he wanted to do was embarrass himself by blowing his load so soon. He wanted to savour the feel of her, but his need for release was fighting with his desire to prolong the pleasure.

"Nope." Grabbing his shoulders she began to move on him.

"So cruel," Damon groaned, a smile lifting the corners of his lips.

She returned his smile and then moaned as she pulled up and slammed back down onto him. The head of his shaft stroked her inner wall as she began to rotate her hips in a circular motion as she moved on him. The car was tight quarters, but they made it work.

"Your cock is so good. I love it," she gasped, brushing her lips along the side of his neck.

Her covered breasts brushed against his chest as she moved. He longed to remove her dress completely to get a full view of her stunning breasts, but this wasn't the best locale. He'd indulge himself when they got home. He'd indulge in every inch of her beautiful body when they got home.

In the background, he could hear the cars as the whizzed by the station. If one stopped, they'd be discovered and the thought only increased the excitement of the moment.

Letting his head fall back against the seat, he began to thrust up into her as she moved up and down on him. He was getting closer, at the point where he doubted he'd be able to hold back if he tried. He opened his eyes and watched her. Her eyes were closed, her back arched and judging from her expression and the tension in her body, she was getting close. She was becoming so wet that her juices were seeping from her and dripping onto his lap and coating his rock solid balls.

"Come for me Kat. Milk my cock baby!"

She couldn't respond as the grip on his shoulders tightened and her soft whimpers and moans became louder and more frequent. The muscles of her pussy tightened their grip on his throbbing cock as she prepared to release. His balls became tighter, preparing to unload his seed into her needy core.

Wave upon wave of pleasure came rushing through him and he was becoming light-headed. He became single-focused, he needed release. Now! A dozen cars could have driven up to them, their drivers watching and he wouldn't have cared less at this point.

"Oh yes, yes, yes!" She cried out as she gyrated on his lap, moving harder - faster! Her pussy trembled around his throbbing, ready, and loaded cock and she screamed out a final time as a gush of her juices greeting his rock hard member.

The sweet rush of her juices in combination with her cries of pleasure and release did him in. As her pussy continued to tremble and explode in a series of orgasms, he reached his breaking point, pulling her down hard onto his cock as he thrust up. He groaned his release as a stream of his cum began to fill her, beating against the walls of her pussy and mixing with her juices. She collapsed against his chest, burying her face against his shoulder, panting hard.

Damon released her hips and slid his arms around her, holding her tight to his chest, nestling his face into her rose scented hair. "Oh damn. Kat, honey," he groaned as a final shot of his cum unloaded into her, leaving him completely sated, as the mixture of their fluids surrounded and seeped down his cock and onto his balls.

"You feel so good," Katrina sighed, placing a light kiss on his neck. He didn't have a chance to reply as her body jerked up and she began to scramble from his lap. Her knee nearly missed nailing him in the groin as she threw herself across the seat and into the passenger seat.

"What in the fuck, Kat?"

"Car, car, car!"

As the words came from her mouth he noticed the headlights of the car coming from behind them. "Ahhhh dammit! You have got to be kidding me."

Katrina frantically wiggled in her seat as she pulled down her dress. "Afraid not. And I was so looking forward to being bent over the hood."

Damon grinned as he glanced at the police car rolling up behind them. "Of all the broken down service stations in all the state they have to check behind this one? Seriously?" he grumbled under his breath as the officer stepped out of the cruiser and approached the Lamborghini, a flashlight focused on Damon and Katrina.

The officer, a tall, lean, young man barely out of the academy, Damon suspected, stepped up to the driver's side and glanced from Damon to Katrina and back again. "Licence and registration."

Having already pulled the required information out of his wallet, Damon passed them to the officer who glanced down at them, without really reading what was on them.

"May I ask what you two are doing back here?"

Damon didn't think it was that hard to figure out considering the deep blush colouring Katrina's cheeks and her mussed up hair and make-up, but he didn't make that remark.

"Well, Officer. My fiancé had a little too much to drink at a charity function we just left and needed to pee." He rolled his eyes and shrugged as if to say. *You know women...*

"Have you been drinking, Mr. Garratt?"

Damon shook his head. "Not a drop." And that was the truth. He'd been drinking more than he should lately, not that anyone would blame him considering the circumstances, but the urge to drink was pretty much non-existent now.

The officer clucked his tongue off of the roof of his mouth and nodded. "Good enough. Have a good night, Sir." He nodded towards Katrina. "Ma'am."

Damon waited until the officer was in the patrol car before starting the Lamborghini. He glanced over at Katrina and smiled. "Good God woman. Will you stop getting me into trouble!"

Laughing, Katrina gave him a soft slug on the shoulder. "Ass."

Chapter 14

"Why won't you just tell me where we're going? This is crazy!"
Laughter from Damon was her only response. The bugger was
enjoying her suspense. She hadn't needed her passport so she ruled
out any out-of-country destination as their wedding locale, but the
United States was a big place. A very big place.

"You'll know in less than ten minutes Kat. I will tell you this.
Once the plane lands we're going to a wedding boutique, getting
your dress, and then tonight we'll have the ceremony once they
have the alterations done to your dress."

Katrina smiled as she settled back into the leather seat of
Damon's plane and tightened her grip on his hand. It was hard to
believe that only five days ago she was barely making rent, without
a hint of a love life and no real hope of her future getting better.
Now here she was sitting in a private plane with Damon, praying
that it was going to be the start of a long life with him.

She'd decided to be optimistic. She couldn't imagine life being
so cruel as to bring them together just to take him away in less than
a year's time. No, she was determined that regardless of the odds
the doctor gave him, he was going to get through this and they
would have the happily ever after they both deserved.

"At least let me peek out the window." Katrina stood and was
about to brush past Damon to open the blind covering the small

plane window when Damon grabbed her waist and pulled her onto his lap.

"No way, sweetness."

"What will a little peek hurt?" she protested, attempting to get up from his lap, only to be pulled back down again. She wiggled in his arms and felt his shaft harden under her bottom. Suddenly looking out the window was forgotten as other activities became her main focus. She was about to lower her lips to his when the voice of the Captain came over the speakers in the cabin informing them to take their seats and buckle up.

She groaned her displeasure as Damon laughed, while releasing her so she could take her seat next to him. "Just when things were about to get interesting."

"What? You haven't found my company interesting until this point?"

She rolled her eyes at him, fastening her belt. "You know what I mean."

"I think I can make the descent a little more interesting." Damon placed his hand on her bare thigh, just under the hem of her short blue jean skirt. His hand began to slowly inch its way up towards the apex between her legs. As his hand cupped her mound and his fingers slipped into her panties, searching out her increasingly wet heat, what was going on outside became the least of her concerns.

*****

"This is amazing! Vegas? Really?" Katrina attempted to contain her excitement as they exited the airport and headed towards the black Escapade that Damon's secretary had ordered the previous day for them. It was no wonder Damon had been so busy the other day and left her to her own defences at the ranch for so long. He'd planned a lot.

"Really," he confirmed.

"So are we going to be married by one of those Elvis impersonators?" The idea was both tacky and extremely cool in her mind. They used to joke when they were young that one day they were going to elope and get married by Elvis, not because they were fans, but because it was so perfectly tacky and fun that it suited them. Or at least it had back then. Looking over at the new Damon - or Damon 2.0 as she'd nicknamed him - in his black button down shirt and jeans that easily cost a month's salary at her old job, it seemed a little out of character.

"Would I do something so tacky for our wedding Katrina," he asked, his face unreadable as he unlocked the Escalade and opened the passenger side door for her and motioned for her to slip in.

She frowned, not entirely sure as he closed the door behind her and made his way around to the driver's side of the vehicle.

"You know, I'm really shocked you're not blacklisted from renting a vehicle considering the condition you returned the Ferrari in," Katrina commented as he slid behind the wheel.

Chuckling, Damon started the vehicle and pulled out of the parking slot. "It was only a few scratches."

"A few dozen gouges. And don't forget the dent."

"I still say that dent was there when I picked it up."

"Uh-huh. So where are we heading now?"

Damon didn't respond until they were leaving the airport and headed for the hub of Las Vegas. While he'd been close-lipped on most of the plans, he did inform her that they were staying in a suite at *Caesars Palace*. That was exciting all in itself as far as she was concerned.

"We're going shopping. Getting you a wedding dress and then tonight is the wedding. We should have some time to do a little gambling if you want before the ceremony."

"Ceremony done by Elvis?"

Damon ignored the last question.

She didn't have a chance to ask any more questions as she became distracted by the casinos and bustle of the people around them. People ranging from homeless to those wearing ten thousand dollar suits walked the sidewalks as they drove down the strip.

"We should go see a David Copperfield show," she commented as her eyes spotted a billboard featuring his face and advertising his show.

"Whatever makes you happy babe." He slowed the vehicle and parked in front of an elegant bridal boutique. The dress in the front window caught her eye straight away; an off the shoulder Victorian styled dress with layers of ruffles, beads and lace.

Damon's eyes followed her gaze and he smiled. "Found it already?"

"Don't know yet." Not waiting for him to get out and open the door for her, Katrina opened her door and hopped out of the Escalade and made her way into the bridal boutique. There were hundreds of stunning dresses on racks and on display, but the dress in the window called to her. Walking to the front window, she fingered the white satin and lace.

"It's Vera Wang. Beautiful isn't it?"

Katrina heard the soft voice of the sales lady behind her and nodded, not bothering to look.

"It would look stunning on you. Would you care to try it on?"

Vera Wang, aren't those rather expensive? She was about to say no and continue to look, but Damon stepped in.

"Yes. Please. She'd like to see how it fits."

"Damon..." She was about to protest, but she loved the dress. Trying it on wouldn't hurt. Right?

"We have a duplicate out back that I think will fit you, follow me please."

Katrina had the urge to protest a second time, but the dress was so beautiful. She had to at least try it on. Damon was smiling down at her when she lifted her eyes to meet his. She was about to protest to him that it would be expensive, but thought twice, knowing what his response would be to her protest on a money basis.

"This way, Ma'am."

Katrina followed the middle-aged, yet strikingly beautiful sales clerk into the dressing room.

"If you need any assistance, please let me know," the sales clerk said, hanging the dress up on the wall exiting, closing the door behind her.

After stripping down to her panties, Katrina grabbed the dress. Not being able to resist, she looked at the sales tag pinned to the back of the dress. Twelve thousand dollars! *Unless this makes me look like a Goddess I'm not getting it*, she silently vowed stepping into it and pulling it up.

She began to pull the zipper up on the dress, but got halfway and was in dire need of assistance. Shit. She flung open the door to see Damon leaning against the wall, one ankle crossed casually over the second. A wide smile broke out on his face as his eyes swept over her.

Her eyes went wide as her mouth dropped. "Damon, you shouldn't be outside the door. It's bad luck to see me in my wedding dress before the wedding."

"Oh, come on. I'm only here to help, now turn around and let me help with the zipper."

The damage was done she supposed. Spinning around she lifted her hair and waited for him to zip her up. Damon stepped up to her back and she resisted the urge to lean back into him as he gently tugged the zipper up and the bodice tightened around her torso and breasts. The bodice fit well, but if she gained even a single pound it would be too tight around the stomach, but all-in-all it was a nice fit. As good as it was going to get without being altered. She stepped up to the three-way mirror as she released her hair, letting it cascade down her back.

"You look stunning. Like a fairytale princess." Damon said walking up to her and placing his hands on her shoulders and catching her eyes in the mirror.

"I think you're overstating a bit."

"I don't."

Her mind flashed back to their prom. She'd worn a pink princess gown and insisted that he wear a matching pink cummerbund and bow tie.

"What are you grinning about?"

"Our prom."

"The pink cummerbund and tie?"

She nodded. He'd fought with her for days over having to wear pink, but she'd won out in the end.

"You wanna know a secret?"

Her grin widened. "Of course. Love secrets."

Reaching into his pants pocket Damon pulled out his wallet, flipped it open, reached inside and pulled out a well-worn photo, crumbled at the corners.

"That's not..." Excitement bubbled within her. She still had some pictures of the prom, but they were packed away in her mother's attic. He passed it to her and sure enough, it was. Two grinning, younger versions of themselves looked back at her.

"I can't believe you still have this and you carry it with you?"

His face reddened as he nodded. "Yeah, I do." He shrugged. "Memories."

"All these years, always with you?" Her eyes remained glued to his. *Oh God, not again*, she groaned inwardly as the tears threatened to appear in her eyes. She'd never laughed or cried or felt so many emotions in such a short period of time in her life as she had with him in the past five days. It was like an emotional rollercoaster, but it was good.

His face reddened further and he cleared his throat. "Yeah." He shrugged. "You know... It..."

She nodded. "I know. Damon-"

A knock at the dressing room door interrupted them, spoiling the moment. Damon stepped away from her and opened the door for the sales clerk. "We'll take the dress, can you have a couple of alterations done by seven tonight?"

The clerk beamed. "Of course! We have a stunning matching veil."

"Then by all means, let's see it."

*****

Damon pulled Katrina against his side and kissed the top of her head as they waited their turn at the *Graceland Wedding Chapel*. "Last chance, we can have our wedding in Bangor if you want."

She shook her head and looked up at him. "Not a chance."

Katrina looked radiant. Happy. The look of love and admiration in her gaze filled his heart. There was no doubt in his mind this had been the right decision. In fact, it was easily the best decision he'd ever made in his life. He'd fucked up when they were young, but at least they were able to make it right. He just had to win this cancer battle. She deserved more than a year. She deserved a lifetime of happiness and he'd do whatever treatment traditional, non-traditional or otherwise to give her the life she deserved.

The chapel doors burst open and a young happily married couple that was lucky to be over the age of twenty burst through the doors. Music flowed from the chapel and the Elvis minister followed behind the couple, exiting the chapel. The Elvis minister who looked nothing like the real Elvis approached Damon and Katrina.

Oh Damn, this is so tacky, Damon chuckled to himself, but glancing down at Katrina it didn't matter. She was smiling ear to ear, embracing the tackiness of the situation.

"Katrina and Damon," the minister asked as he approached.

The nodded in unison.

"You kids ready to get hitched at the Graceland Wedding Chapel?"

They nodded in unison a second time, and then looked at each other, both fighting to keep from laughing out loud at the craziness of it all.

"Then follow me. You got the plus package right. The plus package includes photos of your glorious union into marital bliss and photo key chains."

They exchanged amused grins behind the ministers back as they followed him. Katrina's arm linked with Damon's as they walked towards the wedding arch, walking to an alternate fast tempo beat of *Here Comes the Bride*.

"Are you sure you want to do this here?" Damon whispered to her as they approached the arch. She nodded enthusiastically.

Laughing, Damon shrugged. "Okay. You're the boss."

"Ooooh, I like the sound of that," she whispered back.

****

Katrina didn't hear much of what the Elvis minister was saying; her focus was on Damon. Her heart was racing and she felt like a giddy schoolgirl. This was easily the craziest thing she'd ever done and she couldn't be happier about it. He looked so handsome and, from time to time, he'd looked down at her, catch her eyes and give her a sexy heart-stopping grin or wink.

"I'm told that you both have written your vows," Elvis stated glancing from one to the other.

"We have," Damon confirmed.

"Then by all means, Katrina would you please say your vows."

Once they finished with getting their marriage licence the previous day, they'd separated to different parts of the house and took several hours to write their vows. Katrina had gotten up several times during the previous night to make adjustments to hers while Damon slept. There was so much that she felt and wanted to say, putting it into a few lines of prose seemed to be an impossible task.

Damon lifted her veil and pushed it back so they could look eye to eye without the thin white barrier and then took her hands in his. As their eyes locked, to her horror she realized that she'd forgotten her lines. She hadn't brought her lines with her and with a silent curse she realized she was going to have to wing it.

He frowned, "Are you okay Kat?"

Katrina nodded and gave him a nervous smile. Taking a deep breath in, she slowly released it and began. "Damon, I spent years looking for the one person I was meant to spend my life with, but he never showed up. I realized when we reconnected at the reunion that the reason he never showed up was because I'd already had him - he'd been you all along. You knew me better than anyone when we were young and that hasn't changed despite the years that have passed. I loved you back then and I love you now and I'll love you on our fiftieth wedding anniversary. I know we have a rough road ahead, but fate brought us back together for a reason. You're my Price Charming. You always have been and always will be. I love you."

Oh God, that was awful, she groaned inwardly.

Elvis smiled and nodded towards Damon. "And Damon, please give your vows."

Katrina could see the nervousness in him as he took a deep breath in and released it. She squeezed his hands in reassurance. "Katrina, you know that I've spent years being consumed with all the wrong things. It has taken me a long time, and a huge wake-up call to see that I had what was most important in life a long, long time ago. You mean more to me than anyone on this earth ever has or ever will. I feel fate jumped into our lives to bring us back together and do now what we were meant to do a decade ago. I promise that I will devote the rest of my life to making you happy and giving you the family that you want and deserve."

His eyes were so intense and so sincere that it made her eyes tear up. Releasing one of her hands he wiped the tears away as they ran down her cheeks. "Baby, I'm going to get through this. *We're* going to make it through. Now that I've found you again there's no way in hell I'll leave you so soon. *No* way. We're going to grow old and grey together, no matter what it takes. I promise you Kat."

The tears began to flow freely and a confused Elvis stepped back as she threw herself into his arms and buried her face into his neck. "I can't bear the thought you losing you Damon. I can't. It's too soon. It's not fair. I won't let you go, I won't!"

Damon pulled her tight, placing a kiss at her temple, attempting to soothe her. "I'm not going anywhere sweetie. Nowhere. I mean what I said. We're going to beat this and we'll be spending the next fifty years fighting, and making love and creating babies. There's going to be years of good and bad and everything in between and we're going to be going through it together."

The Elvis minister clearing his throat made them realize where they were and what they needed to do. Elvis had the weddings set up with twenty minutes in-between each ceremony and they were holding up the line of couples in the waiting room.

She pulled away from him, not even wanting to think about how her make-up looked.

He kissed her softly on the lips and pulled up. "Let's finish getting married so we can start the honeymoon."

"We're getting ahead of ourselves here," Elvis interrupted, "The kissing comes after the rings."

Katrina grinned. "Sorry."

Chapter 15

"I'm perfectly fine of walking Damon," Katrina protested as Damon swiped their room key into the reader and when the green light and beep signalled, opened the door.

"I know you could, but I'm not going to let you." Without waiting for another protest, Damon scooped her up into his arms. Katrina giggled and slipped her arms around his neck, holding tight to him

Despite the grace and ease that he picked her up she noticed him wince as he carried her over the threshold. *Men, why can't they just admit when they need to be taken care of!* While he never spoke of whether the incision still hurt, she noticed that from time to time, like when she'd nudged him before realizing he'd had an operation, he'd wince or flinch, so it was always at the back of her mind.

"Holy shit, this is amazing!" *I seem to be saying that a lot lately*, she mused with a grin as she excitedly looked around the room as Damon kicked the door closed with his heel and proceeded to carry her through the suite, heading for the bedroom.

The suite was mostly black and white and modern and chic in design, nicer than most peoples' condos back in Bangor. Hell, nicer than any of their condos even! It was the type of room you expect to see celebrities staying in. She wondered briefly if anyone famous had stayed in the room before them, but her ponderings were short-lived as Damon reached the massive King sized, four poster bed and placed her onto it.

He leaned over her, kissing her lightly. "So are you happy with how we went about this?"

"It was perfect." It couldn't have been more perfect in her mind. It was exactly how she'd envisioned it when they were younger. It was beautiful in all its cliché brilliance.

He straightened back up and undid his tie. "We can have the huge, extravagant wedding later on if you like."

Katrina huffed. "So we can invite a bunch of people were barely know or like? The only people I'd even be interested in coming was Farrah and my parents. And considering at the current moment my parents aren't exactly on great terms, it seems unnecessary." She crawled to her knees and poofed out the skirt of the dress then proceeded to remove her veil. "Besides, I have the stunning dress. Beautiful rings. And the most amazing man I've ever met or dreamed of meeting. I even have wedding photo key chains to celebrate the event. What more could a girl ask for?"

Shrugging off his tuxedo jacket Damon nodded, a grin spreading across his lips. "Good point. It is all about the dress... and the key chains."

He caressed her cheek, his expression becoming serious. "In all seriousness... Are you okay, Kat?"

Closing her eyes, she took a moment to savour the feel of his hand touching her so tenderly. "I'm okay. I had a little meltdown at the church, but I'm okay now. Chalk it up to wedding stress, that's all."

She opened her eyes, took his hand in hers and kissed it. "Now, no more sappy talk, otherwise I'll be spending our wedding night crying and not performing my wifely duties."

"Oh, yeah, we don't want to distract you from your duties. My apologies." He took a step back eyeing her intently, as he kicked off his shoes.

She felt a shiver run through her at the feral intensity of his gaze and the apex between her legs became instantly wet, beginning to saturate her white lace panties in anticipation of him. She swept her tongue along her lower lip as she motioned for him to come closer as she crawled to the edge of the bed.

He obliged, stepping up to the bed and peering down at her. Katrina undid both of his cuff links, and then reaching up, she began to undo the black pearl buttons on his white dress shirt. As the material parted she began to kiss her way down the exposed flesh.

Damon slipped a hand into her hair and stroked her long locks. The pull of her hair felt divine sending sweet shivers through her, intensifying the throbbing that was beginning between her legs.

"You're body is... It's amazing, Damon. Amazing." She reached the last button and pulled his shirt out of the waistband of his pants. Straightening back up, she slid her hands up his chest, and slipped the shirt from his shoulders. Damon remained still, his fingers slipping through her hair as she fingered the lines of his muscle in his chest and then his abdominals. Her eyes shifted to the scar at his side and she gently fingered it, not allowing herself to dwell on the reason behind it. She kissed his lean stomach and then glanced up at him, catching her lower lip between her teeth as their eyes locked.

Damon leaned down and ghosted his lips across hers. "Turn around honey."

Trying not to get caught up in her skirt she turned on the bed and pulled her hair to the side. Damon slowly tugged down the zipper on the back of her bodice. The fabric slowly fell away from her naked breasts. She lifted her arms over her head and he pulled the dress up and over her head. For a moment she was blinded by white satin as it moved up and over her body and then off, leaving her in only the jewellery set he'd bought her, garter, white nylons, lace panties and white strappy heels.

Damon's lips skirted her shoulder and he nipped at her neck, just below her earlobe. She sighed, letting her head fall back against his shoulder.

"Give me a minute. Don't move." He kissed her neck a second time and stepped back from her.

"Okay," she sighed. Behind her came the rustling of satin and lace as he presumably put away her gown. Her nipples began to tighten due to the combination of the coolness of the room and her increasing arousal. His footsteps came towards her, from behind and with each step the tension and need within her increased.

His arms snaked around her chest and he cupped her breasts, his fingers pinching and rolling her nipples. Short jolts of pleasure and pain rushed through her as he teased her nipples. "I think you're getting ahead of me honey." His voice flowed through her like liquid fire, fuelling her desire.

"Good thing we have all night."

"Ummmm. We do." He fingered her diamond necklace, as he nuzzled the back of her neck. "I think we'll leave this on."

"Whatever you want." She reached up behind her and laced her fingers, behind his neck. Her back arched and breasts jutted forward as she leaned back against him, her head resting on his shoulder.

Capturing her chin in his hand he urged her face upwards, lowering his lips to meet hers. Her lips parted, inviting him in and she sighed against his mouth as their tongues touched. As their tongues duelled, another jolt of pleasure and anticipation rushed through her and she gyrated against his hard chest and stomach, the wetness between her legs increasing.

His hand on her breast lowered, slowly sliding down her stomach to slip under her panties and to cup her wet mound.

"Oh Damon," she moaned, tearing her lips from his as she bucked against his hand, silently praying his fingers would part her wet folds and thrust deep within her.

"What honey? Tell me," he demanded.

Her body trembled against him. "I want you."

"How?"

She smiled and moaned as he slipped a finger between her folds, found her swollen clit and began to stroke her. She bucked against his hand and moaned a little louder. "I... I don't care. Any way!"

"Nope baby. You're going to have to tell me." His eyes gleamed with his desire and her pussy throbbed for him in response. No man had ever looked at her with such intense need and lust. Even when they were young and horny he hadn't looked at her so intensely.

She groaned inwardly. Damn him for being so cruel. Sex talk was hardly her strong suit. "You're being cruel," she protested.

He brushed his lips across hers and pulled back, pulled his hand from her mound and stepped back. She nearly went toppling backwards off of the bed because of the loss of his strong frame behind her.

"Damon!" She turned around so she was facing him and judging from the expression on his face, he wasn't about to let her off the hook so easily.

"So?" A sexy grin touched his lips and he cocked a brow up at her. "What do you want Kat."

She licked her lips as her eyes lowered to the front of his pants. His shaft was fully erect pressing against the cotton trousers. Damn him.

"You don't have to be shy with me. You know that."

She froze for a moment, unsure how to proceed. This was foreign to her. Seeing the look of determination in his eyes she knew he wasn't about to budge on what he wanted. *No wonder he does so well in business*, she mused.

"Alright." She leaned back onto the bed, bracing her elbows behind her, thrusting her breasts forward, spread her legs and pulled her knees up so he could get a good view of her soaked panties. "Come here."

His grin widened as he did as told.

"On your knees."

Damon dropped to his knees, so his upper torso was situated between her legs, his mouth little more than a foot from the apex between her legs.

"You forgot my garter earlier," She chided.

He gave his head a little shake, clucking his tongue off of the roof of his mouth. "Indeed I did."

"Remove it."

Grabbing the garter he was about to jerk it down when she stopped him.

"No."

"Huh."

"Not like that."

Damon frowned. "Then how?"

"With your teeth." She was beginning to get into this. She felt oddly powerful; the feeling of control was exhilarating, fuelling her desire.

His frown evaporated and the hint of a grin pulled at the corners of his lips as he leaned over her and his lips brushed across her lower stomach, just above her panties before lowered to her left thigh. He caught the white frilly lace between his teeth and jerked it downwards. She wasn't sure if it was more arousing or amusing as he pulled and tugged - hands free - attempting to remove the garter. Once the garter reached her ankle, he straightened and pulled it all the way off, tossing it to the floor.

"Alright. Now remove my shoes."

Her shoes were removed quickly and as he reached to unhook the top of her nylons from her garter, Katrina stopped him. "Did I tell you to do that?"

Damon chuckled. "No, Mrs. Garratt."

"Oh, I like how you say that." *Mrs. Garratt*, God she loved being called that. She'd imagined being called Mrs Garratt countless times when they were young. She'd even scribbled it on her notebook, as young girls do, just to see how it would look. Katrina Garratt. Yes, she liked it. *It* fit. *They* fit.

He stood and leaned over her, his lips brushing against hers. The smell of his aftershave drifted to her nose, enticing her to move closer. "Mrs. Garratt," he whispered against her ear. She shivered and let her head fall back, her golden hair cascading down her back and puddling on the blanket.

His lips kissed their way along her jaw to her neck. She moaned softly as his lips moved down her neck, sending wave upon wave of anticipation through her. She spread her legs further apart, attempting to relieve some of the tension.

"I don't think I said you could do that," she murmured as his lips worked their way across her collarbone and down the valley between her breasts.

"Nope. You didn't. I'm winging it." His mouth swept over her left breast and then her right, capturing the tight bud between his teeth. A jolt of pleasure raced through her and she cried out, the throbbing between her pussy increasing.

"Damon. Please. Oh my God, I need you."

"Uh-huh," he murmured as he swirled his tongue around her second nipple, before sucking it into his mouth. The coil of desire tightened within her, his teasing was both wonderful and frustrating.

"I need more. Please."

"I see." He released her nipple and began to string kisses down her torso and to his stomach.

"Oh yes. Yes, lower. Please lower."

Once he reached the top of her panties, he stopped and began to kiss the exposed flesh of her inner thigh, as he unclasped the top of her nylons from the garter. Once undone he slowly rolled the stocking down her leg as he kissed her ivory skin as it became exposed.

Once the first stocking was off, he began with the second. Katrina watched in anticipation and sexual frustration as he repeated the process with her second leg.

"Please, please, please!"

His fingers swiftly undid her garter and pulled it down and over her hips, leaving her only in her lacy panties. Hooking his thumbs into the waistband of her panties he took his time to pull them down her legs and toss them to the floor with the growing pile of clothing.

Katrina fisted the blanket under her as she waited, while tempted to beg him to hurry, but knowing he'd only tease her longer if she did. He seemed to be cruel like that. Once she was completely naked, spread wide for him, his eyes caught hers.

"Now tell me," she could hear the tension in his voice. He wanted to plunge his cock deep within her as much as she wanted him to, but his willpower was much better than hers it appeared.

"Make me come." She closed her eyes and let her head fall back again, waiting to feel his lips and tongue on her most intimate of parts.

He leaned over her again, and she tensed up as he began grazing his lips over her shaven mound. "Tell me how you want to come."

Oh dear God! She eyes flew open and she lifted her head, her eyes locking with his. "With your tongue. Please, Damon. Fuck me with your tongue and then give me your cock. I need to feel you come in me. God, please!" She could feel her cheeks burning at her brazen admission.

He chuckled softly. "Was that so hard?"

Yes! She screamed inwardly, but had no chance to reply verbally as his fingers spread her pussy lips and his tongue swiped the length of her from her anus to her clit. She groaned and squirmed against his mouth and his probing fingers as they plunged deep with her. His tongue began to flick and tease her clit as he slid two fingers in and out of her core, stroking her inner core with each stroke.

His tongue and fingers were bringing her towards a climax at an alarming pace. Her elbows holding her torso up became shaky and so she let herself fall back onto the mattress and her hands gripped his shoulders, urging him on. She was getting closer and closer, so close that her body felt as though it was humming, while her juices were slowly slipping from her entrance and down her ass. She needed more, harder and faster.

"Use your tongue!"

Another bout of soft chuckling as he did what he was instructed. He removed his finger and thrust his tongue into her. She cried out, her fingers digging into his bare shoulders as she bucked against his mouth and a wave of pleasure and relief washed over her as she came into his mouth.

But Damon was far from finished and was intent on keeping her riding the high of her climax. As the evidence of her orgasm greeted his probing tongue, he continued to tongue fuck her pussy, his fingers pinching and rolling her clit. She bucked and moaned against his mouth, lifting her head to watch him, his face buried between her legs.

It was good. Too good. *Oh-my-God*! Another rush of pleasure raced through her to explode between her legs, making her cry out. Her heart was beating so hard it felt like it was going to explode within her chest as she quickly lost all train of thought and gave in to the continuous flow of pleasure.

Just when she thought she couldn't handle one more second of the glorious sensations racing through her, Damon pulled back, stood up and finished stripping off his clothing. Grabbing her legs, he pulled her towards the edge of the bed until her bottom was hovering over the edge. Stepping up to her, he ran the head of his cock up and down the length of her, taunting her of things to come.

Katrina wiggled against him, attempting to impale herself on him.

"Damn Damon. Give it to me!" She cried out, arching her back and fisting the blanket under her.

Her request was granted as he slowly pushed into her. He took his time sinking into her wet and throbbing core. Propping her torso up with her elbows behind her again, she watched as his cock sank into her. God, it looked so good seeing him slide into her. She wasn't sure what she found more pleasurable, the feel of him stretching her cannel or watching him disappear within her.

They moaned in unison as Damon finished sinking into her, taking her to the hilt.

"Oh yes. So good," he gasped.

They began to move together, Katrina watching as his dick coated in her juices disappeared and reappeared from within her. With each inward stroke the tip of his cock stroked her inner wall, at just the right spot to make her buck and moan against him. She quickly began to ascend the summit once more.

"Come down here." She needed to feel his warm, hard body against her. She needed every part of him as close to her as humanly possible.

He grinned and lowered his torso to hers, crushing her breasts against his massive expanse of a chest.

"Better?"

"Much," she confirmed, slipping a hand behind his head and forcing his lips to hers. He felt good - sooo good - as their bodies gave and took pleasure from each other. Damon pulled his lips from hers and brushed his lips up and down the side of her neck. She arched her back and slid her hands to his back, her nails digging into the rigid muscle.

She wrapped her legs around his waist, pulling him tighter into her and working in time with him, their bodies working in perfect harmony. His balls slapped against her pussy as he began to work her pussy harder, faster. The sensations rushing through her became more intense, and she found herself moaning and crying out with more zeal as she reached the summit.

"I'm coming Damon!" She cried out as her body tensed under him and a gush of pleasurable relief washed over her as her pussy exploded around his shaft, begging him to ride the wave with her.

"Oh fuck Katrina," he groaned, not allowing her a moment to bask in her orgasm as he increased his pace, his dick punishing her throbbing pussy without mercy.

"Yes, yes. Oh fuck me! Yes!" she cried out as she was swept up a second time, her arms and legs tightening around him.

"I'm there. Fuck sweetie, I'm there with you." With a final forceful thrust that moved their bodies a couple inches up on the mattress his cock thickened and then exploded. The force of his cum as it burst from him sent her over the edge a final time and her moans mixed with his and they came down from their sexual high together.

They held each other for a moment, both of their bodies trembling with the aftershocks of their respective releases.

He pulled back and looked down at her, the emotion in his dark eyes so intense it brought tears to her glazed over blue eyes. "I love you, wife."

A wide smile broke out on her lips as she touched the side of his face. "I love too, sweet husband."

"Mmmm, I do love the sound of that coming from your lips."

"Me too." For the first time in her life she held safe, secure; as if everything was going to turn out alright. He was her home, her family.

Chapter 16

"Congratulations on the wedding, Damon." Dr. Van Buren inserted a needle into Damon's arm to freeze the area at his elbow and nodded towards Katrina. "And Katrina. You two look happy. That's good."

"Thank you, Doctor," Damon and Katrina spoke in unison. Damon glanced down at Katrina and smiled at her. She was sitting on the sofa next to him, in his home office in New York, with her hand in his. Damon could feel the stress and tension within her so gave her hand a soft reassuring squeeze. Feeling his hand tighten on hers caused her to glance up and he gave her a reassuring smile.

Gary gave Damon a stern look. "I haven't liked seeing you doing this on your own Damon. It's about time you settled down, it's long past due."

Damon was starting to feel really good about life. Their days in Vegas following the wedding had easily been some of the best in his life. No work - it was a foreign, but good feeling. He'd pushed back all his worries. And he just lived. For a few days he *lived*, enjoying every second. They arrived home the previous evening and now that Monday morning had arrived, it was time to face reality, but he had a much better outlook now. It was going to be alright. There was no doubt in his mind that they were going to get through this and live a long, fun-filled life together. They just had to give over this hump.

"We've already discussed the procedure of inserting the catheter, but I can go through it again if you like."

"Nah, I'm clear on it Gary."

"Alright good. There is one thing that we need to discuss that I don't think we did previously, but it's extremely important giving your situation."

"Sure. Shoot."

"Once I insert the catheter we'll discuss it. You're going to feel a pinch so take a deep breath in when I tell you."

Damon shrugged. "Sure." He glanced down at Katrina and gave her another smile and a wink when she caught his gaze. She looked much more worried than he felt.

"Deep breath in Damon," Doctor Van Buren instructed.

Damon did was told and felt a slight pinch and discomfort in his arm, but nothing worse than a discomfort. Katrina's hand tightened in his. He was actually grateful that she was so worried - in a way - because focusing his attention on settling her down distracted him from his own concerns.

"Alright, we're done. A nurse will be sent to the office to flush and clean it every Monday morning. You can't brush off a cleaning. It's extremely important, Damon, so schedule meetings and such around it."

"Sure Doc. We're going to be staying here in New York until the process is over anyhow."

"Good. Now, I assume you two will be trying to have children?" The doctor pulled his latex gloves off and tossed them into the waste can beside Damon's desk as he packed up his equipment.

Damon frowned. He knew where this was going.

"I would strongly suggest you two see a fertility clinic. Later today if you can, but definitely before the first treatment, because the treatment I have lined up for you will greatly reduce your fertility and there is a very real possibility that it will render you infertile indefinitely. So be prepared for that."

Damon's jaw clenched. It was a blow. A big blow to him, though he suspected as much. It made him even more grateful that Katrina came back into his life when she did.

Gary skimmed through his leather planner, pulled out a business card and passed it to him. I'll call them when I leave and tell them to expect to see you-" He paused catching Damon's gaze. "-this afternoon."

Looking down at Katrina he raised a questioning brow. "Do you want to do this?" He waved the card at her.

Her frown deepened and she nodded, her eyes lowering to their entwined hands. "We should.... In case."

Damon leaned into her and kissed the top of her head. "Okay, set it up Gary. We'll drop in this afternoon and do whatever is necessary. Having a baby is very important to us so however it has to happen."

"In that case, I'll be seeing you in a few days with your first treatment."

"Mr. and Mrs. Garratt, Dr. Robichaud has been waiting for you. Please follow me." The petite blonde receptionist led them down a short hallway, elegantly styled with cream coloured walls and scones on the walls giving off a soft, soothing light.

The receptionist knocked on the door with a golden plate with the name Dr. Ethan Robichaud.

"Come on in."

The receptionist opened the door and led them into a small office, which kept in line with the warm toned theme of the clinic. The man behind the large oak desk, a slender man of his late fifties, extended his hand to first Damon and then Katrina.

The receptionist quietly excused herself from the room and closed the door behind her. The doctor re-seated himself, while Damon and Katrina seated themselves across from him.

"It's good to meet you both. Dr. Van Buren asked that I take special care of you two and that we're on a bit of a time crunch."

"Yes."

The doctor opened a file folder which already contained a number of medical reports. "I've already read through your medical history and am aware of the treatment Dr. Van Buren has planned for you, Damon. So there are a couple things I would like to achieve this afternoon."

"Of course. Whatever is necessary. That's why we're here."

Katrina nodded her agreement and then reached over to Damon and took his hand.

"First, I need blood work from you both. Damon, I'm going to need you to donate today and come back every day over the next several days until your first chemo treatment. Katrina, we're going to do a full medical exam on you, because we'll be starting the insemination process during your next ovulation."

"Now to Katrina, when was your last menstrual period?" He poised his pen waiting for an answer.

Katrina shrugged and crinkled up her nose. "Ummm, a couple of weeks ago, maybe."

Doctor Robichaud looked up from his paperwork, a brow raised. "Maybe?"

"I don't know..." She looked at Damon who simply laughed and shrugged.

"Baby, I have no idea. Not sure why you're looking at me."

When was my last menstrual period? If the truth be known she really didn't know. She never paid much attention to it. To her it was an uncomfortable few days every once and a while then back to life as normal.

"Alright. We'll know everything we need to once the tests are done anyhow. But, I would like you to keep track of it from now on."

Katrina felt an embarrassed blush colour her cheeks at being chastised.

Doctor Robichaud didn't seem to notice her embarrassment as he continued. "So we're going to get right too it. I'll send my nurse in to take blood samples and then I'll do Katrina's examination while Damon gives us his first deposit."

Katrina couldn't help but snicker as she glanced at Damon out of the corner of her eye. It was his turn to be embarrassed at the thought of masturbating into a cup.

"So. Let's get started."

*****

"I swear I've never been so sick of jacking-off in my life Kat," Damon groaned as he plunked himself down on a sterile chair at the clinic, his specimen cap in hand. They'd been advised to refrain from intercourse while he was doing his daily collections at the clinic, but that was near impossible. They were newlyweds for heavens sakes and it didn't help that he got hard every time she brushed up against him, or she looked up at him with desire in her blue eyes.

However, of the past five days, two of those days he managed to restrain himself from indulging in her. Two was better than nothing, right? Besides, even though it was a long shot, he did prefer to impregnate her naturally - if possible.

"At least this time they didn't tote me off to another room for examinations and tests." She took the cup from him and placed it on the small steel table beside the chair he was sitting in. She slowly dropped to her knees, between his legs and looked up at him, her eyes beginning to fill with lust.

Damon's cock jerked alive and began to rise to the occasion as she undid his jeans. He shifted in the chair and pushed down his jeans and boxer briefs giving her full access to his throbbing manhood. Pre-cum was already beginning to form at the tip in anticipation.

Katrina immediately grasped his cock in her hand and began to stroke him, in slow, fluid motions. Damon closed his eyes and moaned softly, her hand was soft, and the pressure she was using couldn't have been more perfect.

"Awwww. Damn Kat. I can't wait until I can get you back home so we can do this properly." He began to thrust up into her hand as she stroked him. The only good thing about doing it this way was that he could be selfish. There was no holding back, no making her feel good - not that he minded. He loved making her feel good, but in this moment there was none of that. All he had to focus on was the end goal, his release and the pleasure that came with it.

Opening his eyes he glanced down at her and could see the strain on her face. She was turned on. Seriously turned on and the way she was eyeing his cock he could tell she was drying to wrap her glossed lips around him and suck him dry. He groaned loudly at the thought. She looked do fucking good with her lips wrapped around him.

"Don't worry honey. I'll make sure we square you up when we get home."

Her gaze lifted from his dick to meet hers and she smiled, a soft seductive smile. "Good. Because I have a number of things in mind for you."

A jolt of pleasure rushed through him, and his stomach tightened. Damon groaned, as he fisted the arms of the chair. He was coming close, really close, really quick.

"Oh fuck yeah. Stroke me harder Kat and be ready. I'm almost there."

She did as told, stroking his length harder, while cupping his balls in her hand, squeezing gently. He bucked a little harder into her hand and his groans became louder, so loud he feared that he might be heard by the other patients in the waiting room down the hall.

He bit down on his lip, trying to keep himself from getting too loud as he hit the summit. If the goal hadn't been to get off as fast as possible he might have been embarrassed by how fast her skilled hand was getting him off, but speed was the goal in this instance.

"Grab the cup, I'm coming Kat," he half groaned, half growled as his balls hardened, his shaft throbbed and a rush of relief washed over him as his seed came spewing from him, and began to fill the cup.

Damon slumped back into the chair and sighed loudly a grin forming on his lips as relief washed over him. "You're right Kat. I much prefer your assistance."

Closing the specimen jar, Katrina slowly got to her feet with a grin of satisfaction on her lips.

Standing and doing up his pants, Damon's grin widened. "Why are you grinning? I'm the one who got off."

"Oh, I'm just thinking about what I'll be getting you to do tonight to make it up to me for my *assistance*." If his cock hadn't been so thoroughly depleted from a week and a half of solid action he had no doubt it would be jerking alive again at the seductive smile on her lips.

"Ohhhh. That sounds... Interesting." Since their honeymoon and him forcing her to verbalize what she wanted, she seemed to let go of her insecurities and now she demanded what she wanted. It was hot as hell.

"Come on, let's do the drop off and have our daily chat with Dr. R."

Damon chuckled as he opened the door and motioned for her and his sample to proceed out into the hallway before him. "I really don't think he'd like to be called Dr. R. He doesn't have much of a sense of humour."

She glanced up at him, as they began to walk towards the reception desk to drop off his sample. "I kinda noticed that. But at least you didn't have him and several hot interns staring at your nether regions."

Laughing, Damon cocked a brow up at her. "Nether regions?"

She gave him a nudge in the side with her elbow. "Well, I can't use your potty mouth bedroom language in a medical facility now can I?"

He didn't have a chance to respond as they were approaching the reception desk. The petite blonde receptionist - who they had come to know as Cindy - stood as they approached and extended her hand to accept the specimen.

"Great. Thanks. Doctor Robichaud is waiting for you guys. If you could proceed to his office that would be super and I'll take care of this for you."

Leaving the reception, they headed to the office that they had become all too familiar with. The office door was open and the Doctor was busy writing something in what Damon presumed to be his chart. With hesitation the couple proceeded into the room.

"Good to see you two." He motioned to the two chairs in front of his desk. "Please have a seat." He clucked his tongue off of the roof of his mouth as he reclined in his chair and eyed them both, his expression impassive.

Alright, this is different, Damon mused, shooting a curious look over at Katrina who seemed to be thinking the same thing.

"I have some interesting news."

Interesting? Interesting good. Interesting bad. Damon frowned.

"As it turns out Mrs Garratt is pregnant."

"With *my* baby?"

It wasn't until he received a not so gentle smack on his shoulder that he realized the words that had come out of his mouth. Looking down at Katrina glaring up at him he groaned inwardly. *Oh fuck, really bad choice of words!*

Chapter 17

"Katrina, no. I didn't... I didn't..." He let out a loud huff and thrust a hand into his dark hair. It seemed surreal. They'd only been trying for a little over a week. It seemed nothing short of a miracle.

"You didn't what, Damon." She'd turned in her chair, her expression blank.

He took her hand in his and brought it to his lips. "I didn't mean to say it that way. It's so fast. It's so... Unbelievable." Standing, he pulled her to her feet and into his arms. "I didn't mean it that way I promise. I know it's mine."

She relaxed in his arms, wrapping her arms around his waist and holding tight to him. To his surprise he felt tears springing up in his eyes. He had it all now. Everything. "I'm so lucky Kat. You have no idea how happy I am at this moment," he lowered his voice so the doctor who was watching on with interest couldn't hear, "thank you Kat. Thank you for giving me everything."

The doctor forgotten, he buried his face into her apple scented hair and continued to hold her. His mind was racing with so many emotions, thoughts, feelings, he needed a minute to get a hold of himself and set it straight. When Dr. Van Buren had told him he may be sterile indefinitely he'd been secretly terrified they may never have a child despite saving and freezing his sperm. But now... Now, she was going to have his baby. He was going to have the heir he'd been desperately wanting.

"Thank you Kat. I love you more than you could ever know," he whispered into her hair, praying he could keep back the tears threatening to escape.

*****

Katrina could barely believe her ears. Doctor Robichaud had said that even when ovulating she would only have a fifteen to twenty perfect chance of conceiving. The chance of him getting her pregnant in that small window of time was a miracle in her book. It gave her faith and hope that things would turn around.

She held tight to him and felt his breath hitch. Even at their wedding he hadn't broken down, but now, hearing the news of the baby had done it for him. So she held him tighter, basking in the feel of his arms around her and comforting him. He'd been such a rock through all of this. He was the one that may be dying and he'd been the one comforting her, now she had her chance to return the favour.

"I love you too. It's a sign Damon. It's all going to be okay."

When he finally pulled back from her, he kept her at arm's length. Their eyes locked. She could see the intense joy and relief in his dark eyes, despite the tears that were brimming his eyes and it tugged at her.

"We're going to get through this. I know it now." And she believed it. She was carrying his baby and it was the miracle they needed to push them through the rough road that they had ahead of them.

*****

"God damn it!"

Katrina's eyes slowly opened at the sound of Damon's frustrated curses. He'd been undergoing chemo for three weeks now - three weeks to go and then radiation treatment. They still had a long way to go, but they were at least halfway through the chemo. The past week they both seemed to wake like clockwork - 7am - and proceed to the washroom to vomit whatever was in their stomachs at the time. If it hadn't been so disgusting it would have been endearing.

Damon's new joke was the phrase that: *the couples that puke together, stay together*.

His comment would usually be greeted with a - fuck you, Damon. Her retort would cause a loud bout of laughter to erupt from him. She'd been pregnant for less than a month and was already getting cranky. The worry and pressure was getting to her, no doubt about that.

Sitting up in bed, she opened her mouth to ask what the problem was and snapped it shut again, as she noticed that roughly a third of his thick, dark hair was littering his pillow. She frowned. They knew he was going to lose his hair and it was finally happening now.

Crawling over to where he was sitting on the side of the bed, leaned forward, his head in his hands, she wrapped her arms around his waist and kissed the back of his neck. It wasn't the fact that he was losing his hair that was bothering him - she knew this. It was just another thing that was making the process real.

"You know, I've always had a thing for bald men," she murmured against his neck, placing a string of kisses from his shoulder to his earlobe.

A smile broke out on his lips and he chuckled softly. "Good thing babes, cause you're about to have a very bald man on your hands."

She slid her naked body from the bed and stretched in front of him.

"So are you seriously trying to entice me knowing our typical morning routine?" Damon teased, his grin widening, as his cock jerked to life and his eyes scanned up and down the length of her body.

"I actually feel pretty good this morning." She glanced over at the antique brass analog clock mounted on the wall - 6am. "Maybe it needs to be seven before I start blowing chunks. So we have a whole hour."

Laughing, Damon thrust a hand in the hair he had left and groaned as his hand became filled with more hair. "You have got to be shitting me."

Grabbing his hand she pulled him to his feet. "Come on, let's get you shaved." Her eyes dipped to his groin which was also losing hair and was nearly bald. A look that she *really* liked. "*All* of you shaved."

Damon chuckled uneasily, his gaze following hers to his halfway erect cock. "Oh, I don't know about that..."

She tugged his hand, leading him to the massive double bathroom off of their bedroom. "Come on. *Please.* You might as well. I've been dying to be with a man who is shaved down there. It's sexy. You're going to lose it anyhow."

Damon groaned. However, it was a groan of resignation.

As they entered the bathroom the motion sensors turned the lights on and she lead him to an armless wooden chair situated by the double sink. "Sit."

Doing as told, Damon sat and watched as she walked over to the double Jacuzzi bathtub and turned it on. Once the temperature was perfect she added some lavender scented bath salts and bubble bath. With the water still running, she opened the cabinet under the sinks and grabbed an electric shaver. Plugging it in she adjusted so it would shave him bald and then walked over to him.

Damon reached for her hips, but she batted his hands away. "Nope, not until we're done."

"You're so mean to me."

Katrina rolled her eyes, flipping her hair over her shoulder and out of her eyes. "Uh-huh." Katrina swung her leg over his lap and settled herself onto his lap, facing him. His shaft hardened to its full potential between her legs and she had to push back the feelings of desire that it was being invoked within her so she could get to the task at hand.

Damon glanced down at her breasts, which in her position were less than an inch from his mouth. "And you're saying this isn't teasing?"

Ignoring him, she wiggled on his lap, his shaft slipping between her increasingly wet folds. Flipping on the clippers she started on the left side of his head and made the first cut, leaving a completely bald strip in his dark hair. She wiggled again, only partially to tease him, but mostly because she needed a better position to make the next cut.

Slowly, his hair began to be fall away. She intentionally brushed her dark, tightening nipples across his lips a number of times during the process. Her teasing got her a low, feral growl in response, but he refused to give her the satisfaction of taking what he wanted.

As the final strip of hair fell away, she leaned back on his lap and turned off the shaver. Placing the shaver on the white marble countertop she evaluated the new, bald Damon. He looked good bald, as good bald as he did with hair, but instead of the boyishly sexy look he had with hair, the bald look gave him a dangerously sexy look. She liked the dangerous sexy, bad boy Damon.

"So?"

She looked down into his dark, questioning eyes and a smile spread across her lips. "You look... *really* hot." She reached between her legs and stroked his rock hard cock until a pebble of cum formed at the tip of his cock. She swiped the cum with her thumb and brought it to her mouth. Sucking her thumb in she licked off the cum, as she watched the fire flare up in his eyes. Just as he was about to grab her to situate her on his throbbing cock, she stood and stepped away from him.

"Oh, come on!" Laughing, Damon fell back in the seat.

"Stay there." Walking over to the tub she turned it off. The water was perfect, the sweet smell of lavender filled the room and a couple of inches of bubbles skimmed the top of the water.

Walking back over to him, she grabbed his knees and parted them. Stepping between his legs she grabbed the clippers and fell to her knees.

"Hell no Kat!"

He was about to stand when she leaned forward and flicked her tongue over the head of his shaft, making him groan. He settled back into the chair, as she took the head of his cock into her mouth. She sucked and swirled her tongue along the swollen head until he was relaxed and fully indulging in the feel of her mouth around him. Once he was fully relaxed she let his dick fall from her lips and turned on the clippers.

"Damn woman, the shit I allow you to do to me. I'm fucking whipped, that's what I am. Whipped."

"It's called marriage honey." Looking up, she caught his eyes and grinned, loving his discomfort. "Ready?"

Taking a deep breath in, he exhaled loudly and nodded waving a dismissive hand at her. "Do what you have to do."

Shit, now how to go about this... Her experience with ball shaving was... well... non-existent. *Maybe I should have Googled the best way to go about this?*

"Okay, what's with the hesitation?"

She pulled back and looked at him, pasting the best innocent look she could on her face. There was genuine concern in his eyes. His frown deepened.

"It's going to be fine."

"Maybe we should let it fall out naturally." He made an attempt to stand, but she grasped his cock and stroked him a moment, settling him back down in the chair.

"Bullied. Pushed around," he grumbled, eyeing her intently.

He tensed as she flicked on the shaver and it began to buzz softly. Deciding to just do it, she started her work on the left ball. She worked carefully and after a minute or so his body began to relax and she worked more confidently until his entire groin area was shaved.

Turning off the clippers she placed them on the countertop and inspected her work. "It looks amazing Damon. You're definitely going to need to keep it this way." Looking back up at him she snickered at his flabbergasted expression.

"Hell no. This is a one time deal."

"Oh, come on! I shave for you!"

Damon laughed, "You shaved before we got back together woman!"

Katrina huffed and rolled her eyes. Okay, so he had her there... But still. "That's not the point."

They both remained silent a moment, their eyes locked. He growled low in the back of his throat and gave his head a shake. "We'll see."

Chapter 18

He was surprisingly fine with being bald up top and down below. The look of desire flaring up in her eyes as she looked at his shaved balls made it worthwhile. He could get use to it; it wasn't like anyone other than her would see it anyhow.

Happy with his response she got to her feet and began to walk backwards towards the tub. She beckoned him with her index finger to follow. His eyes travelled the length of her stunning body, pausing at her bald mound. If her seeing him shaved was as arousing to her as it was to him, then he'd definitely keep it.

He followed her to the tub, as he was about to reach her, she stepped into the tub giving him a coy look. Damon followed her into the tub and sank into the bubbles. He would never admit it to anyone, not even Katrina, but he loved the relaxing feel of a warm bath and the lavender scent. It was a secret indulgence. He was positive that there were perhaps scores of other men who would also never admit it. Having his beautiful, naked wife with him made the moment even more enjoyable.

He reached up and grabbed her waist pulling her down to him, ensuring he didn't submerge the catheter which was sticking out of his right arm into the water, otherwise Gary would have a fucking fit when he came in the next day for his check-up and next dose of chemo.

She lowered herself onto him, straddling him and pressing her naked body against his. "I think I'm going to love seeing you between my legs, tongue fucking me with your new bald look," she whispered into his ear, nipping at his ear lobe and making his body shiver in response.

"You'll get to see soon enough." It still shocked him how candid she was becoming, her words turned him on almost as much as her body gyrating against him. He'd created a monster and he loved it!

She sat up on him, grasped his cock and aligned him with her opening. She stared into his eyes as she gently lowered herself onto him. The passion in her gaze increased as she took more of his length in. Her soft, wet core took him in, accommodating his girth and begging him for more.

They sighed in unison as she took him in completely. Sliding his hand to the back of her neck, he urged her lips down to his. She placed her hands on his shoulders and began to ride him, as their lips locked. Her pussy clenched around his cock as she began to work him.

Her lips parted, inviting him to play as she began to move on him. She rotated her hips in a circular motion as she moved up and down on him. The combination of their tongues dancing with the feel of her soft skin pressing against him and the feel of her core milking him was bringing him rapidly to his brink. Of course, it hadn't helped that she'd had him in a state of arousal for over a half hour. Stroking, teasing, taunting. She could bring him or climax faster and harder than any woman he'd ever met.

She pulled her lips from his, slipped her arms around his neck and increased the speed she moved on him. Soft moans and arousing whimpers came from her lips as they skimmed along the side of his neck. Threading one hand into her hair, he placed the other hand on her ass and pulled her down to him with each of her downward thrusts.

Her moans became louder, whimpers more frequent. Her body began to tense.

"That's it honey, let go for me," he groaned moving with her, thrusting his hips up and meeting each of her downward thrusts so that he buried himself completely into her channel - balls deep.

She suddenly pulled back, closing her eyes, arching her back and began to ride him in earnest. The water and bubbles began to splash and splatter over the side of the tub from the force of her movements. Her breasts, which were covered in droplets of water and bubbles, jiggled enticingly from the motion. She was like a blonde water goddess at that moment, beautiful, sexy and bringing him so much pleasure it was near painful.

"Oh God yes! Oh yes!" Her pussy tightened around him as she slammed down onto his lap, cried out and hit her climax.

"Keep going," Damon ordered when she began to slow her movements. He was getting close and was desperate to come. Pleasure was beginning to overtake his body, mixed with the intense tension. His balls were beginning to tighten - painfully tight.

Her pussy continued to tremble around his shaft. Each small tremble of her pussy pushed him closer to his own climax. She suddenly bucked hard on him, almost violently, and with a loud cry out her pussy exploded on him a second time.

The gush of her warm juices and the contracting of her core around him was his undoing. He groaned loudly, spewing a slew of obscenities though what he said exactly he couldn't say, as the dam broke and he came inside of her.

They sighed in unison as they both relished the feel of their bodies connected.

After a few minutes, Katrina pulled back from him and caressed the side of his face. "I love you Damon Garratt."

His insides warmed, as they did every time he heard those words uttered from her lips. Anything and everything could be wrong with the world and in his life and those words made it right for him.

"Love you too Katrina Garratt."

"Mmmmm. I love the sound of that."

He cocked a brow at her and smiled. "I love saying it."

"Oh shit!" A frown replaced her smile and she looked in horror at his arm where the catheter was placed.

Damon groaned inwardly and went to thrust his hand into his hair and groaned a second time when he realized he had no hair. He hadn't even noticed that the catheter had pulled out an inch and the wrapping was drenched with a mixture of water and lavender bubbles.

"Well, I guess the good doctor will be making a house call early this week."

She shook her head giving him a wry smile. "Gary is going to so pissed at you."

"Damn good thing I have money, because I have a feeling he's going to rape me financially for this."

*****

~~ *Two Months Later* ~~

"It's been a long haul," Dr. Van Buren stated, opening Damon's file.

"It has," Damon agreed as he tightened his grip on Katrina's shoulders, pulling her tight to his side as they reclined on the black leather loveseat in Dr. Van Buren's office. Normally the meetings were done at his house in New York, but during the radiation treatments and on this occasion they were forced to travel to the clinic so they could speak to both Gary and the woman who took care of the radiation treatment, Doctor Vivian Rodrick.

Long haul, however, was hardly the term he'd use. It has been a marathon of hell, and Damon thanked God each and every day that Katrina came into his life when she did. She thought he did a lot for her, constantly chastising him for spoiling her, but whatever he did for her was nothing to the strength she gave him. Destiny was definitely on his side where meeting up with her again was concerned.

He looked down at Katrina and could see the worry and fear in her eyes. Not something he liked to see. She'd aged in the previous two months. The stress in combination with the morning sickness was getting to her and it broke his heart.

With his free hand he grasped hers, lifted her hand to his mouth and kissed her knuckles. This got her attention and she looked up at him.

I love you: he mouthed.

Her body relaxed slightly, and he saw the first smile of the day cross her lips as she mouthed: *I love you.*

The sound of Dr. Van Buren clearing his throat broken them from their moment and both sets of eyes became glued to him.

"So I have the results from the MRI and your blood work."

"And..." Damon prompted. *Why in the fuck is Gary beating around the bush? Am I cured or no?*

"I just want to make this clear that the results could change-"

"-is it gone or not Gary," Damon broke in.

A hint of a smile lifted the corners of Gary's lips and Damon's spirits lifted.

Gary held up a hand, "Just hear me out. When looking at the MRI results and blood work the cancer has receded and appears to be gone. But, you have to keep in mind that it can come back. I want to see your ass in here every three months for the next couple of years *at least* to ensure it stays that way. It has roughly a five year window to return before we can technically say you're cancer free. We got lucky, we caught it early. We don't want it sneaking back and catching us with out pants around our ankles." Doctor Van Buren's smile widened. "But all-in-all I feel confident in saying it's gone."

Damon closed his eyes and fell back into the cushions of the love seat, pulling Katrina with him and gathering her into his arms. The relief he felt was like nothing he'd ever experienced. It felt like he was given a second chance, and he'd be damned if he'd ever take what was most important in life for granted again.

*****

The relief that Katrina was feeling was so intense that tears began to flow freely down her cheeks as she fell into Damon and held tight to him, burying her face against his neck. His shirt quickly became saturated with her tears as she fought to get herself under control.

"Hey, it's good news. Crying is for the bad stuff," Damon teased, speaking softly as he captured her chin and lifted her eyes to meet his.

She sniffed and wiped her eyes with the back of her hand. "Crying can be for the good stuff too," she defended, a smile emerging on her lips. "These are tears of happiness. Besides, I'm pregnant I'm allowed to be emotional."

He leaned down and kissed her lightly. "Good point." He ran his fingers through her hair, soothing her.

"Better."

"So much better," she confirmed.

The two doctors across the room were forgotten for a moment until the sound of Doctor Van Buren clearing his throat had them both turning their attention to him.

"So Katrina," Gary began.

Katrina nodded. "Yes Doctor."

"I need you to make sure he does what he's supposed to do. You have to make sure he makes his follow-up appointments. It has been known to come back, so we're still not out of the woods."

Katrina squeezed his hand and glanced back up at him, her smile wider than ever. "You bet Gary."

They were being given a chance and they were going to be a family. There was no way in hell she'd allow him to jeopardize their future to throw himself back into work like he had all his life. Not that he would. He'd been true to his word when they got married. He still spent a fair amount of time running the company, more than a normal person, but he wasn't as consumed as she suspected he once was.

Now, she and their child had become his new obsession and she doubted it would ever change. If any good came from this experience it brought them together, stronger than they ever were before. She'd been spending the past ten years searching for her Prince Charming and come to find out she'd had him all along.

~ Epilogue ~~

6 1/2 months later

"Faster, faster! For the love of God Damon why do you have a Ferrari if you don't know how to drive it!" Katrina screamed as she doubled over in the passenger seat, clutching her abdomen.

If he wasn't scared of getting punched he would have cracked a joke, so instead he only smirked and continued to drive, weaving through the dense New York five o'clock traffic heading for the hospital.

She screamed again, spouting off a slew of obscenities.

"Breath honey, breathe. You know like in Lamaze class." He attempted to demonstrate the technique and was thanked with a slug to the shoulder. He winced. It hurt. She seemed to have gained inhuman strength over the past half hour that she'd been in labour.

"Fuck you. You did this too me. And not only did you have to give me one, but two. Two Damon! Leave it to you to be the overachiever!"

He couldn't hold his laughter back any longer. He sympathized with her pain, but damn it, she was a hoot and a half when she was angry. If he wasn't so concerned over her and the babies - twins it seemed - then he would have been horny over the fire that was in her blue eyes.

"We're using condoms from now on buddy. Your sperm is potent and there's no way in *hell* I'm going through this again!"

As it had turned out, the chemo hadn't fully killed his boys. His sperm count was seriously down, but Dr Robichaud was convinced that in a few years his numbers would be back to normal.

She screamed again and her hand shot out and grasped his leg. Her fingernails tug into his thigh through his black suit pants. He winced, but didn't say anything.

He'd been in the middle of a business meeting when he'd gotten the frantic call from her. He'd left the meeting with Kevin heading it up. Kevin had proved to be invaluable over the previous few months and Damon planned on rewarding him for his loyalty. When he'd first found out about Katrina, Damon had feared it would challenge his loyalty to Damon and the company, but Kevin had been loyal. The cancer was still gone and life was falling into place so perfectly that Damon doubted he could have been happier.

Except for the pain that was intensifying in his leg... Damn, she'd gotten strong!

He let out a sigh of relief at the sight of the hospital coming into view. "We're here honey."

She lifted her eyes and fell back into the seat. Rubbing her stomach, the contractions seemed to lessen and she regained a slight resemblance to the Katrina he knew. She released his leg and took a deep breath in, releasing it slowly.

"I'll drop you off at the emergency entrance and park the car."

She glanced over at him and shook her head. "Hell, no. I'm not going in alone. I can walk from the parking lot with you."

Damon was about to protest, but the look in her eyes told him to shut his mouth and do what he was told. Being the dutiful husband he murmured, "Okay, sweetie."

*****

"Final push and it'll be all over."

Katrina grunted, tightened her grip on Damon's hand and gave the final push. Moments later a second cry filled the room accompanying the cries of the first baby that was being passed to Damon. Katrina released his hand so he could hold their daughter and watched as they cleaned up the second baby before passing the crying child to her.

As she held tight to what she considered her miracle baby she glanced up at Damon and their eyes locked. She'd never seen so much love, pride and joy in his eyes; not when they were married and not even when he'd received the news that he was cured.

"They're beautiful," one of the nurses gushed, Katrina didn't bother to look and find out which nurse. She glanced down at the baby in her arms, an exact replica of the one in Damon's arms. The babies had bright blues eyes with a tuft of blonde hair on her heads.

"Just like their mother," Damon commented, giving Katrina a smile. Taking her hand, he brought it to his lips and brushed her knuckles across his lips. "I love you."

"Love you too honey," she replied.

"Have you decided on names yet?" Katrina broke her gaze from Damon's to glance at the plump brunette nurse posing the question and nodded. "We sure have."

"What are they?" The nurse's smile widened and it was contagious. A wide grin spread across Katrina's lips as she glanced back down at her baby.

"Faith and Destiny."

"That's so beautiful," the nurse gushed.

Katrina nodded and her eyes caught Damon's again. The names were painfully appropriate. It was nothing short of a miracle that they found each other and conceived their girls when they did. She couldn't imagine calling them anything else. The past ten months had been a rollercoaster of emotion; laughter, tears, anger, but in the end it was worth every second of it. She had everything she could have ever dreamed of and it was all because of her high school sweetheart, the smoking hot billionaire, Damon Garratt.

The End

Excerpt From

Bought And Paid For

By

Terry Towers

<u>Available Now</u>

Chapter 1

Happy birthday, dear Cameron. Happy birthday to you! The chants of her co-workers rang in Cameron's head repeatedly - as if on a sound loop.

Yeah, right, Cameron growled inwardly as she twisted the cap off the wine cooler in her hand, carelessly tossing it onto the kitchen counter.

"Fucking birthday. Who needs it?"

Cameron Seacrest had just arrived home after spending the evening with a small group of her closest friends and co-workers. Tonight was her thirtieth birthday. Various people had told her, over the past month that her thirties were the prime of her life. Everything was supposed to come together like a much-anticipated gift, wrapped in a pretty pink bow; at least that was the myth she'd fallen for in her early to mid-twenties.

How wrong they were; in fact, that wasn't nearly the case.

Sitting down at her desk chair, she swivelled around and turned on the computer. She immediately checked her emails and was shocked to see the number of responses her ad had received. She did a quick count and discovered there were over three dozen potential suitors in her inbox.

"Wow," she murmured, taking a drink from her wine cooler. She set to work scanning the contents of the emails. The goal of her ad was simple - finding the perfect sperm donor.

Owning a successful nightclub and having a beautiful house made her the envy of most women, including some of her closest friends. However, the most important part of life for her had not happened just yet – she was still very single and lonely. All her life longed to be a wife and mother. Until now, she'd been focused on her career driven by her desire to be successful. She couldn't do anything about the husband part, all she could do was hope that eventually her prince charming would appear, but she *did* have control over the mother part and she was determined to make it happen.

She'd spent over a year considering her available options - adoption and insemination, being at the top of the list of considerations. After a while, she managed to narrow down her somewhat long list, choosing insemination.

Determined to meet the man who would help give her what she so desperately craved, Cameron published the personal ad. She no longer *wanted* a baby, she *needed* one, even if the man she chose had nothing more to do with either of their lives other than to donate the sperm in one or more -hopefully steamy - nights of passion.

Her ad was offering two thousand dollars upon verification of pregnancy. Of the very few people who knew of her decision it had become a running joke. Being the owner of a hot nightclub gave her opportunity to have her pick of hundreds of men each night that would be more than willing to give her as many nights of passion that she wanted for *free*.

However, Cameron's gut instinct told her this was the best way; that as soon as she read his email and saw his picture, she'd know him. Most of the men who went to her club were in their early to mid-twenties, more interested in partying than anything else. Cameron wanted a man who was focused, driven - and tall, dark and handsome wouldn't hurt either.

Running a hand through her thick chestnut brown hair, Cameron opened the first email.

"Oh.... No, no, no." she murmured as he introduced himself as a nineteen-year-old, fast food supervisor with a goal of one day becoming a manager. The next could have won the award for "Nerd of the Year." His hobbies included World of Warcraft and D&D tournaments.

Cameron shook her head, not off to a good start.

"Oh dear lord!" Cameron exclaimed, her eyes widening with disbelief as she watched a self-made video of a man masturbating. She took a long swig from her cooler as a stream of cum went shooting from the tip of his cock coating his lap and hand.

Cameron continued to go through email after email. With each email she dismissed, for various reasons, her hopes began to dwindle. Maybe this wasn't such a good idea after all; perhaps she should have sought the assistance of a professional. Maybe her instincts were wrong. After deleting the last email in her inbox, she sighed and sunk back into the black leather computer chair, feeling slightly defeated.

The sound of a loud ding caught her attention and she focused her gaze back to the computer screen almost immediately. There was a new message in her inbox. Was this her lucky man? Cameron's heart raced in anticipation as she opened the new email.

The message was from Sam Jerkins; her eyes immediately went to the three pictures that he'd sent of himself in the attachment. Each one was better than the last and excitement began to bubble within her, along with the light throbbing between her legs at the thought of having such a gorgeous man inside of her.

Her favourite picture was of him on the beach. He' just gotten out of the water so droplets of water glistened on his well-defined, broad chest under the sunlight. His blonde hair was short, and his eyes were smoky blue-grey. He was looking directly into the camera, drawing her in. He looked like he belonged in Calvin Klein underwear commercials.

Chewing at her lower lip, Cameron silently prayed that this man was for real and not some high school kids' idea of a fun prank. Closing her eyes and taking a deep breath, she let out a long sigh before going through his message.

Dear sperm seeker. Cameron laughed at being addressed as the sperm seeker, which she supposed was true. *I was considering writing an entire email selling myself to you. However, I'm thinking the best way to decide whether we could be a perfect fit for this endeavour is for us to sit down for a coffee, in a place of your choosing, and discuss the proposition you are advertising. I will say upfront that I am a perfectly healthy and extremely active thirty-four year old male, with no major mental or physical issues within my family tree - to my knowledge. By all means, give me a call at the number listed below if you're interested in seeing if we have a connection.*

"Hmmmm, wow." There was no doubt in her mind that she wanted to see if, in person, he was as amazing as she suspected he would be. His phone number was at the bottom of the email in the signature field.

Picking up the phone, she started to dial the number and then froze. Was she really going to do this? Taking another deep breath in, she exhaled loudly and nodded her head. Yes, she was.

Gathering up her courage, she punched in the remaining numbers and listened as the phone connected and began to ring.

"Yeah?" A deep male voice answered.

Cameron's heart fluttered and she silently cleared her voice. "Hi there. I'm calling for Sam."

"Sorry babe. He's not here. You just missed him. He just left for the graveyard shift at the hospital. Is there a message?"

Cameron froze. "I ummm..." She didn't expect to have someone else answer the phone. There was no way she was going to explain who she was and what she was calling for, to this stranger. "No, thanks."

After saying a brief good-bye, she hung up the phone and looked back at the computer screen, deciding her next plan of action. She quickly typed a message with her phone number, requesting a date, time and location for a meeting. Her finger hovered over the **Enter** button for a moment before depressing it and she released the breath she hadn't realized she'd been holding until that moment.

There. Done.

*****

"Morning, bro."

"Morning." Sam shrugged off his leather jacket and draped it over the back of one of the kitchen chairs, and proceeded to kick off his running shoes.

"Coffee?"

Sam looked over at his younger brother Craig and shook his head. "I want to go to bed, not stay up longer. All these overnight shifts are fucking me up. Any calls?"

His brother was the exact opposite of him, both in physical appearance and in personality. Whereas, Sam had short blonde hair and blue eyes, Craig had dark hair that was an inch too long as far as Sam was concerned, and dark brown - almost black -eyes. While Sam was driven and responsible, Craig couldn't seem to care less about bills, career or responsibility.

Craig frowned. "Ummmm. Yeah. Yeah, there was. Some chick. Sounded pretty sexy. Wouldn't leave her name, though."

"Some woman?"

"Yeah. Did you meet someone? She hot?" Craig grinned. "She got a friend? I could stand to get laid, haven't been fucked in weeks."

Crossing his arms over his chest Sam gave scowled over at Craig. "I haven't been laid in seven months. Talk to me when you've gone that long and maybe I'll have sympathy."

"Hey, you're the one working those insane hours. You still haven't answered my question. Who is she? She hot?"

Who in the fuck would be calling me on my home phone...?

"Ahhh. Yeah. I think I might know." Pulling his Smartphone from his pocket, he logged into his email and there was a message waiting for him. Cameron Seacrest. Opening the message, he quickly scanned it, his brother coming across the kitchen to peer over his shoulder at the email.

"You're fucking a girl for cash man?"

"What? Fuck." The last thing he wanted to do was discuss this with his brother when he was so tired he could barely keep his eyes open.

"Well, from what I read you're going to fuck her for cash."

Sam thrust the phone back into his pocket. "It's not quite like that. And I don't know for sure."

"Well, if *you're* not going to do it, then send her my way. I could use a couple of grand. Hey - and if she's hot I might even do her for free."

Sam cocked a brow up at Craig. "The last thing the world needs is a mini Craig running around. I can barely tolerate the original."

Craig snorted, but the grin never left his face. "Well, if you don't do it, you send her my way." Craig grabbed his crotch briefly and his grin widened. "Even if I don't knock her up, I can at least guarantee her a good time."

"You know what. I'm done talking about this. I'm going to bed."

Sam could feel Craig's eyes watching him exit the kitchen. As he made his way through the living room and into his bedroom, he shook his head in mock disgust at his brother's chuckling. Once he woke up from a much-needed sleep, he'd shoot Cameron an email and set up a meeting for the following day.

*****

As she sat and waited at the back of the coffee shop, Cameron's hand shook slightly as she brought the cup of coffee up to her mouth and took a sip. She couldn't believe she was so nervous. This was a business meeting - of sorts. Nothing more or less. She was there to get to know Sam and if they connected, in nine to ten months she'd have the one thing she'd been wanting for as long as she could remember - a baby.

Grabbing her purse from the chair next to her, she pulled her compact out and gave her make-up one final inspection. *God, I hope he likes me.* A soft ding indicating the coffee house front door opening had her averting her eyes from her reflection in the compact to the man walking through the front door.

Oh, my. Cameron's heart rate accelerated as her eyes travelled their way up the man's jean clad legs and past his broad chest to his face. His sexy blue-grey eyes found her dark ones just as her inspection reached his face.

He paused a moment, and then gave her a nod as he made his way across the dining room of the coffee house to her secluded little corner. As he approached, she snapped the compact shut, slightly embarrassed that he'd caught her inspecting herself. Slowly, she rose to her feet extending her hand out to greet him.

"Cameron?" He put his hand out to take hers.

"Sam?" She accepted his hand, and a jolt of electricity shot through her as his hand eclipsed hers as in a firm handshake, that lasted a moment longer than necessary.

"How are you?" Sam asked as a smile of reassurance spread across his lips, helping to ease her anxiety about the meeting.

"I...Um... I'm okay. You?"

"Good." Releasing her hand, he pulled a chair out and sat down.

"I'm nervous," Cameron, admitted lowering her eyes, a faint blush colouring her cheeks as she sat down and laced her fingers on the table in front of her.

His smile turned sympathetic as he leaned forward in his chair and placed his hands over hers. "Now, why would you be nervous? I'm the one being interviewed here."

She lifted her eyes to meet his and there was amusement and kindness in his gaze. His smile was infectious and she found her anxiety slowly depleting as she returned his smile. "Yes, but the nature of what I'm interviewing for is somewhat embarrassing."

"No, it isn't. Now tell me about yourself. Why do you need me?"

To her surprise, he didn't remove his hands from hers and she liked it. His hands on hers were comforting, making him feel more like a friend and confident rather than what he really was - a stranger. An amazingly sexy one.

Her smile widened as she rolled her eyes at him. "Well, I can't very well do it by myself, *now can I?*"

He chuckled. "Good point."

Damn, even his laughing is sexy, she mused.

"So why this way? You're young... Twenty-" His voice trailed off as he waited for her to put the correct number behind the twenty.

"Actually, I just turned thirty."

"Thirty is still very young Cameron."

Cameron sighed. "I know. I know. But it feels like the years are slipping away and if I don't do this soon. *Now*. Then I may never get the chance. I waited for marriage, it never happened"

"So you've never been married?"

She shook her head, a lock of hair falling into her eyes. Before she could brush the strand out of her face, he leaned a little further over and did it for her, tucking the unruly strand behind her ear. The gesture was so sweet, so familiar; it sent a warmth through her, further easing her anxiety over the situation.

"I still think you have enough years ahead of you to not worry yet, but that's just my opinion, it's ultimately your decision to make."

"So why are you interested in umm... donating?"

"Well, both my brother and I are adopted."

"Really?" Her curiosity of him peaked. "Have you met your biological parents?"

"Nope. Don't want to. My brother tracked his down, but I wasn't interested. The people that raised me were my parents. Which makes me curious, have you considered adopting?"

Cameron grimaced. "I have, but being a single woman who runs a nightclub - regardless of how profitable - wasn't preferable in comparison to married couples who also wanted children. I even considered adopting internationally, but once I did my research, I realized this is the best option for my situation."

Sam nodded. "Fair enough."

His thumb stroked her wrist, sending a delicious shiver through her. She had to bite her lower lip to keep from moaning. She'd been so caught up with making her night club a success over the past couple of years that she'd been neglecting her romantic life. The simple feel of his hands on her, and his thumb stroking her wrist reminded her how superb it was to have a man touching her. She squirmed in her seat, trying the relieve some of the tension building between her legs.

Scolding herself silently, she tried to clear the indecent thoughts beginning to race through her mind. "So, why do you want to do this?" Her gaze lowered to their entwined hands. His hands were strong, but unnaturally soft for a man. How would those hands feel caressing her body?

"Well, I'm a resident at the hospital and I'm embarrassed to admit that the med school bills are rather hefty. So the money is a very, very small part of it," he shrugged, "but more importantly, as I mentioned, I'm adopted. My parents tried for years to have children before they decided to adopt. I know how important children are in peoples' lives. If I can help someone with that, then that's reason enough for me."

Cameron lifted her eyes once more to meet his and saw a devilish gleam shine within them and he gave her a wink.

"Besides, it's been an awful long time since I've gotten laid and meeting you tonight makes me pretty confident that I can add another reason to the list of reasons why I would be interested in doing this - with you."

Her cheeks grew hot as a bout of nervous laughter overtook her. She was embarrassed, aroused, amused. A million emotions rushed through her. "Then perhaps you could drop by my place tomorrow night and we could discuss the legal aspects of this arrangement."

"I counter that with the offer to take you out, we can get to know each other better, *and then* we can go to your place and discuss the terms."

Is he asking me out on a date?

"Is it smart to go out on a date when our arrangement is for-"

"I think it's *extremely* smart. It may take a number of tries you know."

She squirmed again. Multiple times with Sam Jerkins? Yes, please. A bout of boldness emerged from her, fuelled by her increasing desire for him. "As many times as necessary."

The electricity between them increased, she could almost hear it crackling in her ears it was so intense. She licked her lower lip, as her eyes lowered to his lips.

"It's a nice night. How about we get out of here and go for a little walk?"

Soft & Hard Erotic Publishing

www.elixaeverett.com

Contact Information

Website: www.elixaeverett.com
Email: terry towers@hotmail.ca
Facebook: Terry Towers
Twitter: TerryTowersXXX

Works By Terry Towers

Available Now - Singles
Frat Party Partner Swap
Hers To Command
Daddy's Special Christmas Gift
All For Daddy (Taboo Edition)
The Marine's Naughty Sister (Taboo Edition)
Little Virgin Sister's Webcam Show (Taboo Edition)
Doing Her For Dad (Taboo Edition)
Deceiving Him (The Billionaires' BDSM Sex Club)
Her Brother, Her Hero
Her 'What if' Guy (Pursued By The Billionaire)
The Inheritance: Anything He Craves
The Game Of Love: House of Sex, Scandal and Sexy Singles
Moan For Big Brother
Moan For Daddy
Milk Money (Lactation Erotic Romance)
Bought And Paid For (Breeding Erotic Romance)
Seduced While She Sleeps
Seducing Big Brother
An Heir For The Billionaire

Available Now - Themed Singles
Taken By The Team (Humiliation And Gangbang Fantasies Fulfilled)
Taken By The Marines (Humiliation, Gangbang And Cuckold Fantasies Fulfilled)

The Cop And The Girl From The Coffee Shop
The Politician And The Girl From The Coffee Shop
The Assassin And The Girl From The Coffee Shop
The Bounty Hunter And The Girl From The Coffee Shop
The Firefighter And The Girl From The Coffee Shop
The CEO And The Girl From The Coffee Shop
The Porn Star And The Girl From The Coffee Shop
The Rock Star and the Girl From the Coffee Shop

Available Now - Series
Hitching A Ride
Hitching A Ride 2: To Trust A Con
Conjugal Visits
Conjugal Visits 2: New Beginnings
Sibling Rivalry
Sibling Rivalry 2: Never Say Never
Sibling Rivalry 3: In It Together
Moan For Uncle
Moan For Uncle 2: Keeping It Secret
Moan For Uncle 3: No More Secrets
Moan For Uncle 4: Skeletons In The Closet
Moan For Uncle 5: Love Or Duty
Moan For Uncle 6: To Love And Honour
Moan For Hubby (Moan For Uncle 7)

Available Now - Mirror Editions
(Please note Mirror Editions are mainstream non-PI editions of some of Terry's bestselling taboo works.)

Doing Her For The Boss (Rewrite of Doing Her For Dad)
The Marine's Naughty Sister (Rewrite of The Marine's Naughty Neighbour)
The Virgin's Webcam Show (rewrite of Little Virgin Sister's Webcam Show)
Seducing Blake (Rewrite of All For Daddy)

Now Available - Bundles
The Terry Towers' Taboo Collection Vol. 1

The Terry Towers' Taboo Collection Vol. 2
Naughty But Nice Mirror Edition Collection
The Moan For Uncle Bundle (Books 1-3)
The Sibling Rivalry Bundle (Books 1-3)

Coming Soon
The Rock Star and the Girl From the Coffee Shop 2: Everything
Changes

Works By Nikki Nexus

Available Now - Singles
Daddy Says: Ménage Sex Games
Santa's Brothel
The Confessional: The Naughty Nuns Series
The Fire Eater
Taken By The Team (Humiliation And Gangbang Fantasies
Fulfilled)
Taken By The Marines (Humiliation, Gangbang And Cuckold
Fantasies Fulfilled)

Available Now - Bundles
Naughty But Nice Mirror Edition Collection

Works By Adrian Athens

Available Now
The Welding Instructor
Melting Point

Works By Elixa Everett

Available Now - Singles
Escort With 1000 Faces
Lust, Love & Luck
I Conjure Thee (Enslaved To The Djinn)
Midnight Encounter - Seduced By A Vampire (Quickie)

Tag, The Vampire's Game
Erotic Flash: A Vampire's Seduction
Children Of The Vampire King (Non-erotic horror)
Claimed and Bred By The Wolf
Claimed and Bred By The Wolf 2: Pack Initiation

Available Now - Series

A Night At Club Vampire
A Night At Club Vampire 2: Nigel
Visions Of The Vampire Queen (Book 1 Of The Vampire Queen Series)

Available Now - Bundles
Vampire Whispers - (Bundle of 4 Erotic Vampire Stories)

Works By Angelique Ambers

Available Now - Singles
Forced Into Submission (Her Fantasy, His Pleasure)
Kidnapped And Dominated (Her Fantasy, His Pleasure 2)

Insatiable Reads Book Tours

Loved the book? Terry Towers is part of Insatiable Reads Book Tours, where the hottest authors in romance debut their sizzling new reads! As one of our author's readers, you qualify for the Insatiable Reads VIP newsletter: sign up and you'll be notified of new releases, giveaways and discounts before anyone else!

To enter giveaways and meet the other writers, follow us at:

Website: http://www.insatiablereads.com

Facebook: http://www.facebook.com/insatiable.books

Twitter: http://www.twitter.com/insatiablereads/

Google+:
https://plus.google.com/u/0/100902224798608127488/posts

Pinterest: http://pinterest.com/selenakitt/insatiable-reads/

If you liked An Heir For The Billionaire, you might also enjoy these books:

Mad for You - Anna Antonia

I had gone to high school with Gabriel Gordon. Despite his heavenly name and matching beauty, Gabriel was anything but angelic. Rich, spoiled, and far too cynical for his age, he could easily charm the skirt off a prim beauty or a young teacher or two. Gabriel Gordon was mad, bad, and ...well, you probably know the rest.

The years hadn't changed him, despite taking over his father's company and expanding it into a multinational corporation. Unfortunately, it was just my luck that I found myself working in Gabriel's building. Although I had managed to avoid him for the better part of a month, a chance encounter in the elevator proved he was still an arrogant man who showed far too much interest in the shape of my mouth and nape of my neck.

From then on, Gabriel bedeviled me, teased me, and more often than not, made me want to throw things at his head. Still, just as in high school, I couldn't help but see the pain behind his lazy grin and the shadows in his crystalline gaze. When Gabriel confessed his love for me, I should have been the happiest woman in the world. Too bad I couldn't believe him...

Emma Adams had always considered herself level-headed, even-tempered, and most of all, sane. So how did she become someone who couldn't seem to push Gabriel Gordon away? No matter how sweet his words could be or how easily passion exploded between them, getting involved with the outrageously wealthy playboy had to be the height of insanity. Given their tumultuous natures and personal demons, there was only way a relationship between them could survive: in madness.

A Bride for the Billionaire - Laina Madrid

Ella Kincaid has escaped the poverty of her youth to become a sought-after music teacher for the children of the wealthy. She loves her work, but can't help resenting the easy privilege and self-assured entitlement that mark her elite clients' lives. The opulence that surrounds her can never be where she belongs.

When billionaire David Russo hires her to teach his young nephew, Ella is drawn to him despite her instinct that getting involved with a rich man can come to no good. Before attraction can turn to love, he forces her into a sham marriage, confirming her worst fears and shattering her fragile trust in him.

David only wants his ailing mother to believe he's happily settled. But he's captivated by his reluctant bride, and before long, pretense isn't enough. Can he show Ella the man he really is, and win her heart before it's too late?

Saltwater Kisses: A Billionaire Love Story - **Krista Lakes**

When small-town girl Emma LaRue won a vacation to an exclusive tropical island, a last minute cancellation meant she would be going by herself. Shy and studious, she never had time to fall in love, and often wondered if she was just meant to be alone. However, that all changed when a handsome stranger literally walked into her life while on the beach and sparks began to fly.

New York's most eligible billionaire bachelor Jack Saunders thought this vacation would be the perfect escape, one last hurrah, before taking full control of his father's company. When an innocent Emma didn't recognize him, he figured that he might get a chance to have a vacation from being rich. He didn't tell her about the cars, the yacht, or the penthouse. All he did was let her fall in love with him.

Soon, Jack found that he was the one falling in love with Emma. When they enjoy a fantasy marriage ceremony on the beach, they thought it was a bit of harmless fun before returning to their normal lives. A bittersweet goodbye was supposed to be the end of their perfect vacation romance, but when photos of the ceremony were leaked to the press, everything changed.

Feeling lied to and thrust into a world of wealth and privilege, Emma must choose between following her dreams or following her heart. Will she be content at being nothing more than the billionaire's wife, or will she return to her normal life with only memories of saltwater kisses?

Tied to Him: The Billionaire's Book and Call, Book 3 - **Delilah Fawkes**

Jackson Pierce is a man with a secret…Becoming Governor isn't in the cards for billionaire and former D.A. Jackson Pierce unless he can squelch the unsavory rumors flying around. He's not ashamed of his bad boy past being a dominant at a BDSM club, but he knows the revelation could ruin his political career before it even begins.

He's skeptical of his campaign advisor's idea--find a do-gooder wife to give him a more respectable image--until he meets Rose Turner, a former foster kid working in a local community center. Compassionate, feisty and passionate about helping troubled youth, she's perfect for his needs. But as they get to know one another, his feelings for her grow all too real.

Rose Turner can't take another heartbreak, not after being abandoned by everyone she ever loved. When she accepts Jackson's proposal, she vows to keep her distance, but the more she gets to know him, the more she wants to let him in. But trust doesn't come easy—if he wants it, he'll have to earn it.

As the two draw closer, threats roll in: if Jackson doesn't flip on education reform, a blackmailer will expose the fake marriage, ruining his career and tarnishing Rose's reputation. But if he gives in, funding for the community center will be cut, and Rose's kids will lose it all. With everything on the line, he must make an impossible decision as the clock runs down. What's a man of principle to do when everything he believes in falls apart?

Bitter Farewell (Brothers of Rock #3) - **Karolyn James**

On stage, Chasing Cross are brothers of rock n' roll. Off stage, guitarist Danny and lead singer Johnnie are actual brothers. However, when their father passes away, their reactions are not the same. They head back to their hometown to pay respects, but to Danny's surprise, Johnnie makes his peace before the funeral and abandons Danny, who for the first time must face his own demons and the place he used to call home.

Olivia is desperate for something to happen... staring at old pictures isn't the same anymore. She regrets never making it out of Bakersville, Virginia, but as much as she wanted to leave, she couldn't leave her aging grandfather. She could never turn her back on him, on their memories, or on the house that contains so many years of their family's life. But inside Olivia feels estranged and alone.

The second Danny sees Olivia, he's taken back to their childhood. It seemed like nothing could stop them... until a wedge was driven between their young romance. Danny shot out of town and to the top of the rockstar world. Olivia stayed behind. Danny swears he won't feel guilty about his life and career... and he swears he won't fall for Olivia again after all these years. With heavy emotions racing through Danny's body, coming home may turn out to be the biggest mistake of his life... or the perfect time to change everything...

www.ingramcontent.com/pod-product-compliance
Lightning Source LLC
Chambersburg PA
CBHW050036180626
46810CB00002B/748